FINDING
THE
Invisible
Woman

HEIDI RENEE MASON

——— HOT TREE PUBLISHING ———

ALSO BY HEIDI RENEE MASON

FINDING THE INVISIBLE WOMAN

HEIDI RENEE MASON

HOT TREE PUBLISHING

For information, contact the publisher, Hot Tree Publishing.

www.hottreepublishing.com

Editing: Hot Tree Editing

Cover Designer: BookSmith Design

e-book ISBN: 978-1-922359-87-2

Paperback ISBN: 978-1-922359-88-9

I AM
BY JOHN CLARE

"I am! yet what I am none cares or knows,
    My friends forsake me like a memory
lost;
    I am the self-consumer of my woes,
    They rise and vanish in oblivious host,
    Like shades in love and death's oblivion
lost;
    And yet I am! and live with shadows
tost."

This book is dedicated to invisible women everywhere —you know who you are. It's easy to lose sight of our true selves in the midst of putting everyone else first.

It's easy to forget the people we once were, those courageous and audacious girls we used to be. It often seems as if we've lost them entirely, but we must work to fall in love with ourselves once again, bruises, wrinkles, imperfections, and all. As Oscar Wilde said, "To love oneself is the beginning of a lifelong romance."

PROLOGUE

HAD I KNOWN THAT DAY IN THE COFFEE SHOP that the conversation I was about to have would forever alter the course of my life, would I have stopped myself? If I could have seen into the future, far down the road to how it would all end, would I have opened my mouth at all? They say hindsight is 20/20, but I'm not sure I believe that. Even now, so many months later, I'm uncertain.

A part of me, the part that was somehow immediately consumed by him, knows the answer is unequivocally yes. I absolutely would have had the conversation, even knowing all that would come after it. I would have had it because I couldn't have helped myself. I was drawn to him like the proverbial moth to a flame. My world spontaneously combusted that day. I couldn't have avoided him if I had tried. But the truth was that I didn't try.

The other part, the rational, logical, responsible part of me says that if I'd had a crystal ball to see into the future, I would not have leapt so easily. I would have proceeded with caution, weighed the risks. In weighing them, I would have chosen the safe route. I would have continued on the same monotonous path, plodding through my days, doing exactly what I was supposed to.

That conversation, one brief moment in time, just a small blip on the radar of my life, sparked the incessant questions that plagued me every day after. Questions like *am I happy? Is there more to life than this? Can I live in the same rut for another twenty years? How did I end up here?*

They turned out to be questions I wasn't ready to answer. If I had thought about what might happen, more than likely I would have stayed inside my own small world, continuing to take up as little space as possible, afraid of reaching too high for fear of rocking the boat.

But on that day, just an ordinary Tuesday in October, he stepped in line behind me and commented on my shirt. The shirt was nothing special, just a blue blouse I had worn a hundred times. It was completely unremarkable. Yet he remarked on it. He noticed. He saw me. In doing so, he upended my world, the aftershocks sending me on a path that turned out to be anything but ordinary.

The conversation between us is one I've played over and over in my mind every day since. We sat at different tables, adjacent to each other, yet somehow kept finding things to say, reasons to talk. Eventually he stood and walked to my table, sliding into the seat across from me as if he had every right to do so. I didn't object. I didn't tell him not to. Truth be told, everything about the gesture made perfect sense. Being in the presence of the stranger at my table felt as comfortable as slipping into my favorite pair of worn-in jeans.

Conversation wasn't something that had ever come easily for me. Small talk made me nervous. I would almost rather cut off my right arm than discuss the weather. I usually preferred to listen rather than speak, and it took me forever to warm up enough to share my thoughts. I don't know what spell he cast to crack me wide open, but whatever it was opened the floodgates. I sat at that table and told him things I'd never told anyone; secrets I hadn't even shared with my best friend.

While we talked, it seemed that time stood still.

We were in a bubble, he and I, and nothing else was real. Everything I had been up until that moment ceased to matter. I wanted to be whatever he thought I was, because the woman I saw reflected in his eyes was not the dull one I knew myself to be. I was lost in his world, and I wanted to stay there forever.

Finally, I glanced at my watch and realized we had been talking for over two hours. Reality crashed into me like a wrecking ball, destroying the brief moment in time we'd created together. I stood abruptly, knocking over the chair in my haste. With trembling hands, I grabbed my purse, practically running from the coffee shop. I didn't look behind me, knowing if I did, I would never leave.

Something about the magnetic pull of him wanted to hold me there, caught in his force field. Oh, how I wanted to remain in his orbit! I knew in that instant if I didn't break away, I'd never be able to. So I ran from the coffee shop, racing away before gravity pulled me back.

I jumped in my car and raced toward home, tears streaming down my face and sobs racking my body. I felt as if I'd left a chunk of my heart lying on the table before him. All I wanted was to go back, to sit there basking in the peacefulness of his presence. The depth of his calm blue eyes convinced me that he could put my shattered pieces back together again.

But I didn't go back. I reminded myself that women like me didn't do things like that. Instead, I pulled into the driveway of my house, wiped my face, and went inside to prepare dinner. After all, I was a forty-three-year-old mother of two. I was someone's wife, wrapped so completely around my husband and children that I had lost all sense of my own autonomy. I had virtually ceased to exist outside of them. But that was the life I had willingly constructed for myself, and even in that pivotal moment, I couldn't bring myself to regret it.

And yet that man, a perfect stranger, looked deeper into my soul than anyone had in a very long time. Maybe no one had ever seen me like he had. It made me want to simultaneously vomit and break into laughter. He had sent me reeling. He had shattered my benign existence. In a mere two hours, he reminded me that I wasn't invisible.

Truth be told, I've thought of him ever since. I even went back to the coffee shop at the same time every single day for a month, just hoping to see him again. But I never did. Eventually I tried my best to wipe the encounter from my mind, although I've yet to forget the way he looked at me. The mere thought of him still makes my heart skip a beat, yet I don't even know his name.

But those giddy sensations are just precursors to the guilt that plows into me when I admit to myself how much that man consumed my thoughts in the days that followed. That guilt has made me realize I am an awful person.

After all, what kind of wife can't seem to exorcise the vision of another man's face from her mind? What kind of wife harbors unresolved feelings for that man, a man she spoke to for only two hours? What kind of wife keeps such a secret from her husband, never telling him that his isn't the face she sees when she closes her eyes?

Unfortunately, I've since learned the answer to that question—she's the kind of woman who deserved everything that came crashing down on her after that ordinary October day.

CHAPTER ONE

ONE YEAR LATER

Trees blurred past my peripheral vision as my SUV sped down the freeway. Glancing at the GPS, I realized we were nearly there. I kept my hands on the wheel, telling myself it was too late to turn around. The anxiety that had knotted my gut for the past few weeks gripped a bit tighter. I tried to unclench my jaw and relax my shoulders, but the tension held tight.

"We're almost there, right, Mom?" Stella, my twenty-one-year-old daughter, spoke quietly, glancing up from her phone.

"We are," I sighed deeply. "Don't you remember?"

"No, I don't remember much about the place at all," she replied, her forehead creasing.

"I don't suppose you do. It's been twelve years since we've been back," I said, speaking mostly to myself.

Of course, Stella remembered virtually nothing of Cottage Brook, my hometown. She had only been there a handful of times, and the last time was twelve years ago. She was just nine. Her sister, Celeste, two years older, probably had a better memory of it, although I wouldn't say hers were especially good. Most of my mine were ones I would prefer to forget. I'd spent all of my adult life trying.

"How does it feel to be back, Mom?"

Stella ventured a glance at me, tucking her long strawberry blonde hair behind her ear. Worry lines creased her pretty face, her milk chocolate eyes filled with compassion. She was such an intuitive, sensitive, artistic soul, always able to pick up on my moods and emotions with ease. I had to tread carefully with Stella, as she could so easily absorb my feelings and make them her own.

"The jury is still out on that one, babe. Let's just say that I am not in any hurry to get there." I gave her a lopsided grin, attempting to lighten the mood. Stella didn't need my baggage weighing her down. She had her own grief to work through.

"Do you think Grandma will remember us?" Stella ventured.

"I don't know. The doctor says she has her good days and her bad ones. It seems a bit hard to tell," I answered, drumming my fingers on the steering wheel as I chewed my lip.

Truth be told, I had no idea what to expect when I saw my mother. She'd been diagnosed with dementia, but I didn't know the full extent of what that meant. I hadn't had a clue about her illness until a couple of weeks ago, which was really no surprise because my mother and I hadn't spoken to one another in twelve years.

When her doctor called, I was shocked, surprised she'd even told them she had a daughter, seeing as how she'd so thoroughly deleted me from her life. Or had I been the one to sever our tenuous relationship? The exact circumstances of our last encounter were fuzzy in my mind, and I wasn't sure if that was because of time, or because I could so easily compartmentalize the painful things from my past.

At first, not having a relationship with my mother was painful, but as the years passed, living without her toxicity in my life had become a welcome reprieve. My father was dead; not that it mattered, since he had never been around anyway. I was an only child, so I supposed the doctor calling me was some sort of last resort.

When her doctor said I needed to go to Cottage Brook and figure out what to do with her, I'd reacted in the only way I knew how—I threw my cell phone across the room, shattering the screen in the process. After that I'd screamed as loudly as I could, my body crumpling to the floor as I sobbed. Luckily, I was the only one home at the time. I had always done my best to hide my deeply intense emotions from my family. The girls didn't need to see their mother losing it, lying in a heap on the kitchen floor. Mothers had to be strong, and for me, that meant burying my feelings six feet under and forgetting they existed.

In retrospect, it probably wasn't the most mature way for me to handle the news, but in my defense, I really had more on my plate than I could deal with. I should have stayed on the phone and found out more information about my mother's health. I should have told the doctor I would be there right away. I should have taken it upon myself to play the role of the responsible daughter, even though that was the last thing I wanted to do.

But I did none of those things. Instead, I'd

pushed aside the life-changing news I'd just received, picked up my broken phone, and headed to the phone store, pretending nothing was wrong. I shoved all of the feelings about my mother, the repressed emotions threatening to bubble to the surface, deep down into the blackness where they needed to live. Boxing up the pain was the only way I knew to survive. Ignoring everything else, I went to purchase a new phone.

Should I have done better? Probably. But at that moment in my life I just didn't have the emotional bandwidth to react in an appropriate manner. As it was, I was barely treading water, and if I'd fully absorbed what the doctor was telling me, I would have gone under. The news about my mother was just another blow to my already shattered heart. Her illness would have been enough on its own, but the fact of the matter was that my mother's dementia was just a small ripple in the ocean of my problems.

"What are we going to do when we get there, Mom? Are we going to stay with Grandma?" Stella mused, worry apparent in her voice. "We didn't really make much of a plan."

"No, we didn't, did we? I'm sorry, sweetie, I haven't handled things well at all these past few months," I replied quietly, guilt weighing upon me like a boulder.

"I don't mean that. I just mean, you always seem to have a plan," Stella began. "Of course, none of what's happened would have been part of that plan, would it?"

"It certainly wouldn't. If I could change things, you'd better believe I would," I answered. "I would do anything for you and Celeste to avoid this grief."

My brown eyes, mirror images of my daughter's, welled up with tears. I shook my head violently, refusing to let them fall. I couldn't go down that road, not in front of Stella.

"It's not just me. You're grieving too, Mom," Stella returned.

I didn't turn my head toward her, knowing if I saw the sadness in my daughter's eyes, I would never be able to contain my own. My heart broke for both of my children. If I could take their grief upon myself and spare their feelings, I would do it in an instant. They shouldn't have to go through something so terrible at such a young age.

"I'm not worried about me, Stella. My only concern is for you and Celeste," I deflected.

"Well, I'm worried about you, Mom. And you can't tell me not to be."

"I wasn't going to, because I know that would be pointless." I rolled my eyes and attempted to smile.

"Yes, it would be," Stella quipped. "Because I'm just as stubborn as you are."

"I love you, sweetie. You and Celeste are the glue that's holding me together these days."

I reached across the console and gripped Stella's hand tightly inside of mine, wishing again that I could somehow turn back the hands of time and spare my children this pain. A weighted, heavy sadness had followed us around for months, lurking in corners, permeating the air like a fine mist. A cloud of grief trailed behind the three of us, carrying a foul stench we couldn't shake. I wondered if we would ever be able to crawl out from under the burden of it.

If it was just me, I could handle it. I've learned how to survive the unthinkable, to be strong. I've had to. But to see my daughters in pain was nearly enough to bring me to my knees. My girls were sweet, kind, generous souls. They were innocent. They didn't deserve any of it.

As for me? Well, I'd had it coming. I deserved every single card that had been dealt to me the past few months. You know what they say about karma? Unfortunately, I do. I understand the concept of getting what you deserve better than I ever wanted to. Perhaps I was being hard on myself, but I didn't think so. You see, just six months before I learned about my mother's illness, my husband died, and it was all my fault.

CHAPTER TWO

I SLOWED THE SUV, MAKING THE TURN INTO MY aunt Viv's circular driveway. Putting the vehicle in Park, I turned off the ignition and glanced at Viv's mansion. The white pillars and brick façade took me back to my childhood. I'd always loved coming to my aunt's home. She was strict and proper, but she had always accepted me for who I was, a rarity in my life.

Her home was neat and orderly. A place for everything, and everything in its place was her motto. She had staff to see to her every need, as well as her whims. The chaos that existed in my own childhood home was nowhere to be found in Viv's. I think that's why I had always liked it there. I knew what to expect. The house, like Viv herself, was perfectly predictable.

One look at the precisely manicured lawn and immaculate exterior told me that nothing had changed. Viv was my mother's older sister, and although they didn't get along, she'd agreed to let Mom stay with her until I arrived in town to deal with the situation. The two sisters were not close, and they never had been. Viv and Charlotte, as different as night and day, folks used to say.

As far as I knew, the sisters rarely spoke, so I was shocked when Viv said she would look after my mother until I arrived. Maybe she felt she had little choice, as she was my mother's only relative in Cottage Brook.

"This is your aunt Viv's house?" Stella questioned, taking in the grand home.

"It is. Pretty impressive, huh?"

"It looks a bit intimidating," she mused, her eyes wide.

"Well, wait until you meet Viv. A more perfectly proper woman has never lived," I chuckled.

"But you like her, right? I mean, you've always stayed in touch with her?"

"Yes. She was more of a mother to me than my own. She's a tough cookie, though, so if you're looking for warm and fuzzy, Viv's not it," I explained.

"Why haven't I ever met her?"

"When we came back to visit, it was easier to avoid Viv's house than to argue with my mother about it. And then when we stopped coming back to town, I stayed in touch with her through phone calls. Viv and Grandma hate each other. Or maybe I should say your grandma hates her," I answered with a shrug.

"Grandma seems to hate everyone," Stella observed with a smirk.

"Truer words have never been spoken, sweetheart." I sighed. "Let's go inside."

Stella and I walked to the front entrance, and I rang the doorbell. Inside, the sound chimed like a gong, echoing off the high ceilings. Biting at the skin around my nails, a habit I had never outgrown, I pushed down the need to vomit. I wasn't worried about seeing Aunt Viv, but the thought of dealing with my mother again was almost more than I could stomach.

It wasn't long before the front door opened and a maid ushered us into the immaculate foyer. The marble floors gleamed, and the prism of light glistening from the chandeliers was exactly the way I remembered.

"Your aunt is waiting for you in the sunroom," the maid said efficiently. "Follow me."

I stole a glance at Stella, smiling to myself as I observed the shock and awe written on my daughter's face. Viv's house was a spectacle. She was, by far, the richest woman in Cottage Brook. Her husband, wealthy for reasons I had never known or cared about, died when I was a little girl, and she'd never remarried. Viv didn't have children, and it always made me a little sad to think of her puttering around her mansion with no one but the staff for company.

"Ma'am, your niece is here," the maid declared as we entered the room.

Viv placed the book she was reading on the table beside her, a rare smile turning up the corners of her mouth and crinkling the creped skin around her eyes. Her smile seemed out of place, yet also quite genuine. I felt a sudden rush of emotion at her familiarity, almost forgetting my manners and running to hug her. I caught myself just in time and stayed put. Poor Viv would have fainted from such impropriety.

"Well, Hadley, my darling, here you are."

Viv stood quickly, her posture impeccable, her spine rigid with a discipline the queen herself would find admirable. Her black hair, streaked with gray, was coiled around itself in a stern bun. Her dress probably cost more than my husband had made in a week, and diamonds and jewels glittered about her hands and neck.

I stood still, allowing her to appraise me, wondering if I would be found lacking as I always seemed to with my mother. I should have known better. Vivian was nothing at all like my mom.

"You are as beautiful as you ever were, my girl," Viv exclaimed as she approached me. "That strawberry hair of yours was always the envy of every girl in town."

"You always said that." I chuckled.

"Because it's true. And I see you've passed those lovely genes along to your daughter, because that's who this gorgeous creature must be. She is the spitting image of you at that age, Hadley."

A grin broke out across my face, and I felt comfortable for the first time in weeks. Forgetting everything except how good Viv always made me feel, I stepped forward and hugged her tightly, deciding I didn't care if she pushed me away. Not one accustomed to outward displays of affection, she patted my back awkwardly, but held me anyway, as if she knew I needed it.

Pulling away, I wiped tears from my face and gestured. "Viv, this is Stella, my youngest daughter."

"Nice to meet you," my daughter said with a smile.

"It is lovely to meet you, finally. I can't believe you're a grown woman and I've never laid eyes on you, but I suppose that's just one more thing I can thank my sister for," Viv huffed.

"Grandma can be... quite... difficult," Stella offered diplomatically.

"Now isn't that the understatement of the year? I see your daughter has also inherited your tactfulness and need to please," Viv declared, her forehead wrinkling. "That is a quality I wish you'd kept to yourself, Hadley. A woman should only aspire to please herself."

"Thankfully, Stella wants to please people because she has such a good heart, not because she's afraid of her own shadow."

"And what do you do, Stella?"

"I design jewelry. I have an online store," Stella explained.

"My daughter is being modest. She is an amazing artist, and her jewelry shop is doing extremely well. She's so busy I hardly ever see her. She's quite gifted," I boasted. "And since her business is portable, she was able to come with me."

"So, Stella inherited your creative abilities as

well. Why you never did anything with your own talent, I surely don't know, Hadley. You had such big dreams of being a painter," Viv said with a shake of her head.

"My priorities changed. I had children. I needed to be a good mother."

"The two things are not mutually exclusive. You can be a good mother and still be true to yourself," Viv argued, a spark of mischief in her eyes.

I lowered my gaze, not quite able to look at her as she spoke words that so completely hit the mark. I had been grappling with that for the past couple of years—the knowledge that I had completely lost myself in the process of trying to be a good mother. When I had my daughters, the only thing that mattered was giving them what I never had—a stable mother they could count on. It had consumed me, leaving no energy for anything else.

"And your older girl, Celeste, did she stay in Cleveland, or is she with you?" Viv continued.

"Celeste is working. She just landed a position as a lab technician. It's her first solid job since college, and she didn't want to quit already. Since we're only a couple of hours away, she's staying in the house until I decide what to do with it. She may come eventually if she can find work," I explained. "That is, if I decide to stay."

"Do you plan to sell your house?" Viv asked.

"Yes, I'll have to. I haven't worked in years, and there's no way I can handle that massive mortgage on my own. Charlie always took care—"

My voice cracked, and my resolve began to waver. Being around Aunt Viv made me feel vulnerable, and the wall I had worked so hard to construct began to tremble, threatening to crack. I couldn't let it. Not in front of Stella. I was the parent. I had to be strong, above it all.

"I'm so sorry, Hadley. You've been dealt quite a blow these past months, between your husband's death and your mother's illness. It just doesn't seem fair."

"No, it doesn't," I agreed, my chin quivering. "But I'm fine."

"Are you taking care of yourself?" Viv raised one eyebrow, looking even closer at me.

"Of course she isn't," Stella chimed in. "Mom takes care of everyone but herself. She always has."

"Ah, I see nothing has changed then. That's the way with her. Putting on a brave face for the world while she slowly withered away inside." Viv spoke directly to Stella. "I was hoping she'd outgrown that."

"I'm standing right here, you two," I reminded them. "Besides, that's not true."

"It certainly is true," Viv argued.

"It is, Mom." Stella jumped on the bandwagon.

"You act as if I don't know you at all, Hadley," Viv said with a click of her tongue and a shake of her head.

"You know me, Aunt Viv. You were always like a mother to me."

"A rabid wolf would have been a better mother to you than my sister. I never understood why Charlotte was so awful. She's a viper, that one," Viv declared. "She didn't deserve you."

"Well, I'm here to pick up the pieces for my mother." I shrugged. "I'm her daughter, and she's my responsibility."

"You'll do no such thing," Viv demanded.

"What do you mean? That's why I came. I have to take care of her. That's why you called me here, isn't it?"

"Silly girl, I only said that because I knew you wouldn't come otherwise."

"What are you trying to say, Viv?"

"Hadley, your mother stole your childhood from you, and I did nothing to stop it. I will not stand by and see her rob you of the rest of your life as well, not when I have the means to help," Viv declared.

"Help? What do you mean?"

"Your mother has been staying here for a week now. She has her own suite, and I've hired a nurse who is an expert in dementia to see to her every need. She is well taken care of."

"But she can't continue to stay here, Viv. The two of you will kill one another," I protested.

"I think you'll find that Charlotte has changed, darling," Viv said cryptically.

"People don't change that much, Viv. The two of you cannot live under the same roof," I argued.

"Hadley, this house is large enough to get lost in. I could go days without seeing your mother if I wanted to, and I often do. But she has everything she needs right here."

"Then what am I supposed to do? How can I help? I came here to help."

Viv had thrown me for a loop. I expected to be a full-time caregiver for my mother, no matter how difficult that proved to be. As distasteful as it was, I had viewed it as some sort of penance for what I'd done. I hadn't been the best wife, and I'd never been the daughter my mother wanted, but I believed that coming back to help her in her time of need would somehow assuage the guilt I felt for both of those things. The idea of being a caretaker had given me a purpose, and even though I didn't want it, the mission itself had propelled me forward.

"There is something you can do to help, Hadley. Your mother's house is in terrible shape. The bones of the structure are good, but her housekeeping skills have always been lacking. It's basically fallen to ruins. It needs to be renovated. I think your efforts are best used there," Viv stated.

"So I should get it ready for her to go back home?"

"Darling, I don't know what the doctors have told you, but Charlotte will not be going back home. She'll never be able to live on her own. The disease has progressed quite extensively. She won't live in that house again. It will be yours to do with as you please," Viv explained. "I've already spoken to an attorney about it."

"I don't want her house. I hate everything about that place." I shuddered as a thousand disturbing memories caused bile to rise.

"You have every reason to hate it. The worst years of your life were spent behind those walls. But I think this will be good for you. Cathartic, even," Viv said gently.

"How can this possibly be good?" I huffed.

"I'm going to give you some advice, Hadley, and you may do with it what you will. My advice is this—fix yourself as you fix the house. Both things need renovating, and that work is long overdue, my darling."

CHAPTER THREE

I STOOD THERE TRYING TO TAKE IN WHAT VIV was saying, but the words were having a hard time permeating my brain. I had left Cleveland, driven two hours to Cottage Brook, and somehow worked up the nerve to go to my aunt's house to retrieve my mother. As hard as that had been, I'd done it, fully aware that she was my responsibility. Now, Viv was standing there saying that Charlotte would be staying with her, that my mother would never be going home.

On top of all that, Viv thought I needed to fix up my childhood home. It didn't sound hard when she said it, but the reality was that 1223 Blackbird Lane was the entryway to hell for me, the one place in the world I didn't want to be. That house was where the darkness lived, the terror hanging like a threatening thundercloud just above the roof. It was where the demons of my past hid in corners, jumping out to startle me without warning. I didn't want to inherit that house, or even renovate it, for that matter. I wanted to take a wrecking ball to it, or burn it to the ground.

Every time I set foot in it, I became the terrified, wounded little girl who had grown up there. I had tried so hard to bury her, to leave her behind. But the minute I walked across the threshold of Blackbird Lane, that little girl was there, opening her arms to me, pulling me back inside the nightmare.

"Fixing up the house might be fun, Mom. We can do it together."

Stella, who was staring at me with a worried look on her face, interrupted my terrifying trip down memory lane. She knew me well enough to understand that renovating that house was the last thing I ever wanted to do. Her statement was simply to let me know that she had my back, whatever may come.

"Sure. You're right, honey. It might be good," I offered, making myself smile on the outside. After all, I was an expert at putting on a calm face when, on the inside, I was a turbulent mess.

"I haven't been there myself in over thirty years,

Hadley, but I did send my housekeeper and the nurse last week to check it out. They say it's not fit to live in right now, so you can't stay there," Viv instructed.

"I'm sure it will be fine, Viv," I insisted.

"It's not fine, Hadley."

Viv didn't understand. I didn't have the financial means to stay anywhere else. The only reason I had come at all was because I could stay at my mother's house, however traumatizing, for free.

"We'll just clean it up a bit and live there while we work," I stated.

"You are stubborn as an ox, Hadley. You'll do no such thing," Viv argued.

"Look..." I took a deep breath, trying to find the right words. "I'm not exactly in the best financial situation right now. Staying at my mom's house is really all I can afford."

"Money isn't an issue, darling. I have plenty," Viv said with a wave of her hand.

"But Viv—"

"I've already made reservations for you at the hotel in town."

"You did what?"

"It's the Presidential Suite, so there should be plenty of room for both you and Stella. I would have you stay here, but I think you're going to need some space away from Charlotte while you work on the house."

"What—" I stammered.

"Hadley, I'm no fool. I know what dredging up those old memories will do to you. The hotel will be your safe haven, away from your mother and away from the house."

Once again, tears filled my eyes, and I blinked hard, trying to dispel them. Viv had planned absolutely everything. She had recognized my need and acted, taking the reins from my weary, bruised hands and placing them into her own. She had taken control of the impossible situation, understanding that I didn't have the power to do it myself. Yes, she was so much more of a mother than my own had ever been.

"I don't know how to thank you," I faltered.

"There's no need to thank me. You are my niece, and it is my prerogative to spoil you however I see fit. I just wish I had acted sooner." She smiled sadly. "It is my greatest regret in life."

"Okay," I sighed heavily. "Well, I guess it's time to face my mother, then. How is she? I should probably go up and see her."

"You should do whatever you feel is best,

Hadley. You don't have to do anything you don't want to do."

"But I—"

"If you never walk up those stairs to go see her, no one would blame you. You understand that, right? You have every reason to forget that woman is your mother. I absolve you of her, as I should have done years ago."

"You don't know how much I would love that, Viv." My voice shook with emotion. "But I can't. I don't think I could live with myself. I have to see her, if only to prove to myself that I can do it."

"It is your decision, my dear, but your heart has always been too tender for your own good." I swallowed hard over the sandpaper in my throat while Viv continued, "Charlotte is at the top of the stairs, third room to the left." She turned, threading Stella's arm through her own. "Let's go have some tea in the sitting room and give your mother some privacy, shall we, darling?"

Stella looked at me, uncertainty and worry painted on her face. "Do you want me to go with you, Mom? You don't have to do this alone."

"Go with Viv, sweetheart. You can see Grandma next time if you want," I replied with a tight smile.

Dragging her gaze away from my face, Stella

walked with Viv toward the sitting room. I knew my daughter was worried about my reaction to seeing my mother for the first time in twelve years. To be honest, I was worried myself, which was why I wanted to do it alone. I couldn't regulate my emotions around my mother, and I didn't want Stella to see me in such a fragile state. Viv had known I needed to do it on my own.

Taking a deep breath, I ascended the grand staircase, my jelly-like legs quivering, barely able to support my own body weight. I gripped the smooth railing with my clammy hand, not trusting myself enough to let go.

"You stupid girl! Come back here! I'll show you what happens when children disobey their parents!"

I continued climbing the stairs as my mother's angry words played like a horror film through my brain. The memories crept up unbidden. I tried to push them down, but it was no use. They had been set free.

"I'm sorry, Mama. I didn't mean to break the cup. It just dropped." My five-year-old lip quivered.

"You're clumsy and stupid. I told you to be careful with those dishes." My mother's fiery red hair matched the color of her face as she stomped toward me.

"I'm sorry, Mama," I sobbed.

Knowing what was coming, I crouched on the floor, curling into the fetal position and covering my head and face the best I could. Bruises on faces were too hard to explain. I had learned that the hard way.

Preparing my small body for the pummeling I was about to get, I closed off my brain and felt myself drift, far away from that shabby kitchen and my angry mother. I had gotten so good at leaving my own body that I barely felt her fist make contact.

I reached the top of the stairs. Taking a left, I counted the doorways as I plodded slowly toward my mother's room. When I came to the third one, I hesitantly peeked inside. An older woman sat in an armchair in the corner reading a book. I assumed she was the nurse, as she gave off a confident, no-nonsense sort of vibe.

Stepping a little farther into the room, I worked to control my breathing. I let my eyes wander, taking in the immaculately decorated space, ultimately allowing my gaze to rest upon my mother. Forcing my feet to walk across the plush carpet, I begged my legs to support me, fearing they would give out at any moment. Stopping at the foot of the bed, I looked at her.

I wasn't sure what I'd expected, but the woman

lying before me wasn't it. My mother had always been such a formidable foe, the stuff of nightmares. Looking at her in that moment, she was simply a withering old woman. Her once fiery hair was a shock of white, her face seeming to collapse upon itself. The wrinkles had taken over, causing the surface of her skin to look like a crumbling pastry.

She had always been tall and broad, made of sturdy stock, but somehow, she had shrunk, becoming nothing more than skin stretched too thin across brittle-looking bones. I understood that she had dementia, but her physical changes had clearly been happening long before her diagnosis. If I had seen her walking down the street, I wouldn't have recognized her.

The nurse glanced up from her book and gave me a tight smile. "You must be Hadley."

"Yes... er... I am...," I stuttered.

"I recognized you from the picture." She gestured toward the framed photograph on my mother's bedside table. "And your mother talks about you all the time."

"I'm sorry. I can only imagine what she's told you."

The nurse's brow furrowed with what appeared to be confusion. Glancing at the photograph beside my mother's bed, I was shocked. The photo had been taken when Celeste was a baby. I hadn't even known my mother had it.

I vividly remembered that day. I had just finished nursing Celeste, and my mother had gone off on one of her famous tirades about how disgusting she believed it was to breastfeed. No one had ever made me question my maternal instincts like my own mother. Nothing I did was right. She'd made me second-guess every decision I ever made. I remembered the hurt and anger mixing inside me, churning as my hatred of my mother intensified.

Someone, probably Charlie, had snapped the photo at that moment, and to see my face, you'd have never guessed the turmoil bubbling inside of me. My smile was benign, calm, as if I didn't have a care in the world. I had always been such an expert at concealing myself. I often wondered if there was a soul in the whole world who really knew the true me.

"I didn't know my mother had that photo framed." I shrugged, feeling the need to explain my strange reaction to the nurse.

"I found it on her nightstand, in the bedroom at her house, so I brought it here. It's good to have little reminders of important people in her life," the nurse explained.

"Clearly you don't know her very well. I'm not exactly an important person in my mother's life."

I tried to conceal the disdain in my voice. It wasn't the nurse's fault that my mother and I were so dysfunctional. A lifetime of pain was difficult to explain to a stranger in ten seconds or less.

"But you're Charlotte's daughter," she stated.

"That's just genetics. It means absolutely nothing."

"You must be somewhat important if she had the photo in her room," the woman insisted.

I resisted the urge to argue, deciding it was best to leave things alone. Airing my family's dirty laundry wasn't something that brought me great joy. I changed the subject, deciding to focus on my mother's health instead of our broken relationship.

"How long has she been sleeping?"

"She's been asleep for a few hours."

"A few hours? Does she do that a lot? Sleep in the middle of the day?" I realized I knew little to nothing about her condition, but it was probably time to find out.

"Yes, she does."

"Why does she sleep so much?" I asked.

"Apathy and depression are side effects of the

dementia. Plus, her body is worn out. It all makes her quite tired," the nurse explained.

"Depression? I thought dementia made people forgetful, not depressed."

"Every patient is different, but it's not uncommon to lose one's spark for life in cases like your mother's. State of mind is important. The will to hang on is often a deciding factor."

"I know you must find our situation strange, but I don't know anything at all about her condition. How sick is she?" I asked. "She was just recently diagnosed. I only found out a couple of weeks ago."

"Your mother may have been recently diagnosed, but her symptoms are quite progressed."

"Meaning?"

"Meaning that she's had this for many years. I'm amazed she's managed to take care of herself for so long, seeing how rapidly she's deteriorated in just the last week," the nurse explained.

"I don't understand."

"Hadley, your mother is in the final stages of her disease. Her body is shutting down. She's already unable to move on her own, she needs help with all of her daily activities, and she's having trouble swallowing her food. The forgetfulness is just one symptom. This has been going on for a very long time."

I grabbed the footboard of my mother's bed to steady myself. I had thought her diagnosis was new, and that had been bad enough. This was even worse. She'd been sick for years, and I'd never even known. Guilt mixed with nausea inside my stomach, and I worked to keep my breakfast down.

About that time, my mother's paper-thin eyelids fluttered open. She blinked several times and looked around the room, her eyes eventually settling on me. I felt every bit the child as I told myself not to look away from her, not to cower. I bored my eyes into hers, willing her to do her worst.

To my utter shock, the corners of her mouth turned up into a weak smile and she whispered, "Nurse Mary, look! My Hadley has come home to me."

CHAPTER FOUR

I STOOD THERE, STOCK-STILL, TRYING TO MAKE sense of what was happening. My mother had smiled at me. I had expected her to spew hatred all over me, and instead, she looked almost happy to see me. My heart lurched inside my chest, that wounded little girl surfacing for just a moment, the one who craved her mother's affection more than anything else in the world.

"I'm sorry, Mama. Please don't hit me again," I *sobbed as I curled into the corner of my room. "Why don't you love me?"*

"You're a stupid, worthless girl, that's why. How could I ever love you?" she sneered at me.

I shook the memory away, reminding myself what kind of woman she really was. As my outer shell threatened to soften a bit, I chastised myself, telling that little girl not to fall for her act. Because that's all it was—an act. The woman before me might look harmless, but she was a monster.

My mother didn't possess even a tiny shred of human decency. Just because she was sick, that didn't change anything. I wouldn't allow myself to be sucked in just so she could chew me up and spit me out. I refused to give her that satisfaction. I was no longer a child. I was a woman, and I wasn't going to let her put me back in that place.

"Hello, Mother," I said coldly, replacing the wall, brick by brick, around my heart.

"What a good girl you are," she whispered, her raspy voice barely able to speak the words. She closed her eyes once again and drifted off to sleep.

I wiped my sweaty palms on my jeans and began to pace back and forth at the foot of the bed. Nurse Mary returned to her novel, barely reacting.

"Why is she saying that?" I finally snapped at the nurse.

"Saying what?" Nurse Mary asked calmly.

"That I'm a good girl. That she's happy to see me," I answered tersely. "She doesn't believe any of that, so why is she saying it?"

"I'm not sure how to answer your question,

Hadley," Nurse Mary replied. "Perhaps she's remembering better times?"

"There were no better times!"

"But there must have been," Nurse Mary insisted. "It couldn't have been all bad."

"You don't know anything. My mother is a terrible, hateful, abusive woman." My lips trembled to the point that I could barely speak.

I glanced at her, sleeping peacefully, a wisp of a smile on her parched, dry lips. My mind couldn't seem to reconcile my lifelong abuser with the helpless skeleton of a woman lying before me.

"I've got to go— I can't—" I stammered, feeling like a caged animal.

"This is difficult, Hadley," Nurse Mary said evenly, glancing up from her book. "Dementia changes people. Sometimes we must get to know them all over again."

"I know my mother. Even dementia couldn't change that woman. She is pure evil," I argued.

"Then maybe this is a gift," Nurse Mary offered. "Maybe you'll get the chance to see her as someone else before she goes."

"I don't want to see her at all," I spat.

Turning on my heel, I practically ran from the room. Leaning against the wall in the hallway, I put my head between my knees, telling myself not to hyperventilate. *Control, Hadley. Keep it under control. Put it back into the box. Shut the lid. Bury it in the ground.* I pictured myself doing exactly that. When my breathing was moderately normal, I walked to the other end of the hall and into the bathroom, where I splashed cold water on my face.

"What in the world was that? What is she up to?" I whispered to my haggard reflection.

My mother was a master manipulator, but that was quite an act, even for her. I didn't know what game she was trying to play, but I wasn't participating. She couldn't control my life or my emotions anymore. Gathering my composure, I walked slowly down the stairs and into the sitting room, where Stella and Viv were deep in conversation.

"There she is, back in one piece," Viv said with a concerned smile.

"Barely," I replied with a shake of my head.

"What happened, Mom?" Stella's brow crinkled with worry.

"I don't know," I admitted, the tears beginning to spill from the corners of my eyes. "Are you sure you brought the right person home from the hospital, Viv?"

"As I said earlier, Charlotte has changed," Viv answered.

"That's putting it mildly. She smiled at me. She looked almost happy to see me," I offered weakly as I wiped my face on my sleeve.

"It's difficult to take in, isn't it?" Viv nodded in understanding. "She's like that much of the time. Or else she's asleep."

"You mean she's not up there raging against the world? I don't know how to process that," I shrugged helplessly. "I don't even know who that woman is."

"Don't get me wrong, Charlotte can still be as mean as ever. But there's this new softer side that comes out sometimes. Perhaps she's used up all the hatred she had inside and there's nothing else left," Viv explained. "Maybe this is God's way of showing us a better part of her before she goes."

"I don't even know how to respond to that," I stated flatly, the thought of a semi-kind mother completely foreign to me.

"You don't have to respond at all, darling. There are no expectations here. You know that," Viv reminded me.

"Well, I don't know if I'll go see her again," I confessed. "I'm not sure I can."

"You mustn't feel obligated to," Viv added.

Stella stood from her armchair and hugged me tightly, comforting my bruised, weary soul in the way that came so naturally to her.

"Grandma hurt you, Mom. She hurt you in ways you should have never been hurt. If you don't want to see her again, you shouldn't feel guilty about that." My daughter wiped my cheeks with her palms.

"How on earth did you get to be so wise?" I smiled through my tears.

"Because I had the best mother in the world," Stella answered with a sad smile. "I'm just sorry you didn't."

CHAPTER FIVE

Stella slid into the driver seat, and I didn't argue. Clearly, I was in no condition to operate a vehicle. I felt like a dish towel that had been wrung out one too many times. Viv had given Stella the address of the hotel, so she punched it into the GPS and we headed out of the driveway. I stared out the window, the scenery blurring past my eyes. I barely noticed.

Of all the scenarios I had imagined, the one where my mother smiled and was happy to see me hadn't even made the list. I could have handled her hatred much better than her kindness. At least that would have been familiar. I couldn't remember my mother ever smiling at me. Not once. A slap across the face would have been easier to process.

"Are you okay, Mom?" Stella asked, giving me a concerned glance.

"I don't really know what I am, honey." I sighed heavily. "That's not much of an answer, is it?"

"It's better than you telling me you're fine. At least it's an honest answer. That's good enough for me," Stella replied.

"I guess I'm just angry with myself for not knowing she was so sick. Or that she'd be so different," I explained, trying to put my feelings into words.

"How can she be that sick when she was just diagnosed?"

"Because the nurse said she's had this for years," I said, my lip quivering. "Years, Stella. And I had no idea."

"You had no idea because she cut you out of her life. That's on her, Mom. Not on you," Stella insisted.

"But shouldn't I have known? Shouldn't I have kept trying, even if she cut me off? She's my mother. What kind of person doesn't talk to her mother? A terrible person, that's who."

I tried to keep my voice even, but I felt it begin to rise, along with my heart rate.

"Mom, she's toxic, poisonous. Everyone sees that," Stella assured. "No one blames you."

"I blame me," I replied, guilt ripping my heart to shreds.

"Then that's something you need to work through inside of yourself. You have to put that blame in the right place, and it's not on you."

"But— "

"Grandma abused you, Mom," Stella said gently.

"I know, but—"

"Grandma abused you," Stella said a bit more forcefully. "That isn't your fault."

Out of words and out of excuses, I simply sighed. "Yes, she did."

Seeming to sense that I was nearly at the end of my rope, Stella grew quiet. She didn't push. She spoke the words, then waited as they floated around inside the car. She probably hoped they would breach the surface, tunnel through my thick skin, and eventually take root inside of me. My heart had been so completely decimated the past few months that I doubted it was possible for anything new to grow there. It had become a barren wasteland.

We rode the last couple of miles in silence, and when the hotel came into view, I breathed a sigh of relief. I needed to get out of the car, to busy myself with the distraction of unloading suitcases and getting settled into the hotel room. I needed to do anything other than think of my mother, my hopeless financial situation, and my dead husband. I needed to feel something besides the gnawing guilt that this entire situation was my own fault.

Stella pulled into a parking space close to the front entrance. The Lexington Hotel was nearly a hundred years old and had always been one of my favorite buildings in town. It was an English Tudor-style lodge that reminded me of a place where royalty would stay. I had wanted to go inside so badly when I was young, but I never had the opportunity. Now, thanks to Viv, I would be taking up residency in the Presidential Suite for the foreseeable future.

A bellhop approached the car with a cart on wheels and helped us load our luggage. Stella and I followed him inside to the front desk. When the manager realized I was Viv's niece, he practically rolled out the red carpet, offering both Stella and me cold drinks and leading us immediately to the elevator where he personally escorted us to our room. I had the distinct feeling that Viv had probably donated a large sum of money to the hotel at some point in time, given our VIP treatment.

The manager informed us of all the hotel's amenities, then excused himself, handing me his business card and asking me to notify him personally if things were unsatisfactory in any way. When I closed the door behind him, Stella burst out laughing.

"You'd think you were the queen herself or something, Mom," Stella chuckled.

"Viv is well-loved in this town. Or at least her money is." I laughed. "If you want to be treated like royalty in Cottage Brook, just drop your aunt's name into the conversation."

"She's great. I really like her," Stella announced.

"Viv is the best. She saved me more than once when I was a kid," I answered.

"Speaking of great, how about this room?" Stella gestured at the extravagant Presidential Suite.

"It's pretty amazing," I agreed.

And it was. The main room had a living area, complete with fireplace, as well as a kitchen and balcony. There were two large bedrooms off the main area, each with its own luxurious bathroom.

"Maybe we can just live here forever," I joked.

"Wouldn't that be nice?"

"Hiding out in the Presidential Suite and ignoring all my problems? Yes, please." I nodded.

"I think I want to shower and rest for a bit. I'm pretty tired from the drive," Stella announced. "I also need to check my work emails."

"Yeah, I want to get my things settled too. I forgot my phone in the car, so I'll run down and grab that first," I added.

"I'll take the room on the left. Ta-ta for now." Stella giggled and gave a fancy little wave as she headed off toward the posh bedroom.

I grabbed my keys and locked the door behind me. Stepping into the hallway, I sighed, thinking of all the things I had to do and not wanting to do any of them. I'd rather just bury my head in the sand, or at least in the plush pillows of the Lexington Hotel.

Just then, a scent wafted into the air, stopping me dead in my tracks. It smelled like cedar and citrus, and it sent my head reeling. Although the hallway was empty, the fragrance hung in the air, lingering, taunting. It was intoxicating; familiar and foreign all at once. It brought with it an immediate rush of memory and emotion. It took me back a year, to that day in the coffee shop.

I was certain that thousands of men wore that particular brand of cologne, but my mind didn't go to thousands of men. It went to one—the man who had turned my world upside down in only two hours. He was the man I had been simultaneously hoping to find and trying to forget ever since, the one who had sent me down the path that ultimately led to the very spot where I was standing at that moment.

Shooing the memory away, I hopped onto the elevator and rode it down to the bottom floor. Heading outside to the parking lot, I unlocked the SUV, grabbed my phone, and took a look at the screen.

Wrinkling my nose, I scrolled through the notifications. In the short time I had been inside the hotel, I'd had twelve missed calls. Clicking on the icon, I noticed that all the calls were from the same phone number, one I didn't recognize. The unknown number had a Cleveland area code.

"That's odd. Twelve missed calls from the same number, and not a single voicemail," I mused.

Opening the browser on my phone, I googled the digits. I couldn't seem to narrow them down to a particular person or business name, however, there were various complaints from people about getting calls from the random number.

"Weird. Probably a telemarketer or something." I shoved my phone into my pocket and headed back inside.

CHAPTER SIX

The next morning, I reluctantly rolled out of bed and dragged myself into the bathroom. Turning on the shower as hot as it would go, I stepped under the water and let it rush over me. I tried to convince myself to relax, but my mind had other ideas. It was stuck on repeat, reminding me of the problems I couldn't seem to escape.

No money, check. No job, check. Dying mother, check. Dead husband, check. Impending financial ruin, check. Massive load of newly discovered debt, check. Childhood hellhole that is my responsibility to renovate, check. Guilt, guilt, guilt. Check, check, check, my brain rattled, almost smugly.

Try as I might, there was no running away from any of it. I had fallen asleep almost immediately the night before, telling my problems to go away and leave me alone. But standing in the shower that morning, I convinced myself that I needed to come up with an actual game plan. I had to find a way to deal with all of it, one way or another. Hiding out at the Lexington wasn't going to cut it.

As much as I wanted to crawl back into bed, sleeping my life away wasn't the answer, so I decided that I would get dressed and head over to my mother's house to survey the damage. I needed to know what I was working with, and the only way to find out was to face it head-on.

Turning off the water, I grabbed the fluffy bathroom towel and dried myself. I wiped the steam from the mirror and took a long look at my reflection. I had always been told I was beautiful, but I couldn't seem to bring myself to give that description to the woman I saw in the mirror. She just looked tired, defeated, worn out. I imagined the beauty was there too, although it seemed to be hidden well below the surface these days.

Back in the beginning, my husband, Charlie, was careful to tell me every single day how beautiful I was. He liked to tell people that he was first drawn in by my looks but stuck around because of my charming personality. I thought hard, trying to remember the last time he had complimented me. I honestly couldn't remember. Somehow, all the things that were second nature at the start of our relationship had fizzled out by the end of it.

The thought of Charlie caused a huge lump to rise in my throat. It was still surreal for me to think of him in the past tense, even six months later. I couldn't quite bring myself to believe he was anything other than alive, the vibrant man who had always seemed so in control. His ability to rescue me and take care of things was what had drawn me to him in the beginning. I had needed him way more than he ever needed me. I supposed I was looking for a father figure, and Charlie was born for that role.

I closed my eyes and thought back to the first day I saw him. I had been nineteen years old, running down the sidewalk at breakneck speed, arms filled with the lunch orders of my then coworkers. It was my first day working as a receptionist at a law firm, and I had been sent to get food for the entire office. I was carrying far more than I should have been, and I tripped over an uneven spot on the ground.

Drinks, food, and the entire contents of my purse scattered like confetti across the sidewalk on Main Street, as well as all over me. Stunned and embarrassed by my clumsiness, I looked around desperately, hoping no one had noticed. There stood Charlie, dressed to the nines in his perfectly tailored suit, smiling at me, a look of amusement on his handsome face. His beautiful eyes had twinkled with delight, and a bubble of laughter made its way out of his perfect mouth. It sounded like music. He reached out his hand toward me, and I willingly grabbed it, recognizing it for the lifeline that it became. It was almost as if he had known at that exact moment that I would eventually be his and he would take charge of my future.

He introduced himself, helped me clean up the mess, and made me feel a little less like a complete failure on my first day at the office. It turned out that Charlie was an attorney at the firm where I worked. We went on our first date two days later, I put in my notice three months after that, and six months to the day after we met, we were married.

Celeste was born the next year, and Stella two years after. It had all been a whirlwind, and I was swept up in the magic of it. The job that was supposed to be a temporary stop on my way to art school turned into something else entirely. I plunged headfirst into my future with Charlie, never once looking back.

Until last year, I never thought twice about my

decision. I had gone along with each and every step, constructing a life I never thought possible. For years I was happier than I ever dreamed. I had my husband, my daughters, and my own little slice of heaven. I never thought too far ahead. I never needed to. My life was planned out according to the needs of my husband and daughters.

Given my traumatic childhood, that stability was exactly what I wanted. In fact, I craved it. I vowed to give my children the sort of life I never had. My only goal was to be a good mother. And I had been. All thoughts of art school were quickly pushed aside when I first held Celeste in my arms. I threw myself into the role of motherhood with a zeal I didn't know I possessed. Everything else quietly faded into the background.

Charlie, ten years older than me, was more than ready to be a father, and he had been happy to be my husband. He took care of the major decisions, such as finances, and I took care of the girls. It worked for us. Until it didn't. Somewhere along the way, I lost my identity completely, and it seemed that Charlie forgot why he fell in love with me in the first place.

As our daughters grew older, Charlie and I grew apart. It seemed we had nothing in common anymore, and it had become easier to skate around the issue than to face it. Charlie was a good man, and I loved him, but that spark we had all those years ago had fizzled out entirely. We didn't argue; in fact, we rarely talked about anything important at all. We lived parallel lives, side by side in the same house.

It took a random conversation with a complete stranger to jolt me from my complacency and startle me back to life. After that day in the coffee shop, I wasn't the same, and eventually Charlie noticed. He accused me of having an affair. I told him that was ridiculous and stormed out of the house. After driving around for hours, it finally hit me that Charlie wasn't too far off the mark.

Of course, I wasn't actually having an affair, but my heart was captivated, consumed by a complete stranger. My body hadn't been unfaithful, but my mind had certainly strayed. Nothing was the same between Charlie and me after that. We went on in that state of limbo for months, barely speaking to one another. Then, once again, we had a huge argument. For the second time in our marriage, Charlie accused me of having an affair.

I'd never know what possessed me that morning, but for some reason, I confessed to it. I laid it all on the line. I told Charlie there was another man. I honestly didn't have a clue why I said it, because clearly the man was only a fixture in my mind. But still, I told Charlie I was having an affair.

The look on Charlie's face still haunted me. It was a mixture of complete shock, devastation, and sadness, as if he had only wanted me to deny it, and instead, I confirmed his worst fears. Without another word, he stormed out of the house, jumped into his car, and sped away.

Two miles down the road, Charlie ran a stop sign and plowed head-on into an oncoming bus. He died on impact. He died believing I had been unfaithful. He died without ever realizing I hadn't really cheated on him. I loved my husband, and he died because I killed him.

CHAPTER SEVEN

"Stella, I'm going to head over to Grandma's house now."

I poked my head into my daughter's room but stopped speaking when I noticed she was on the phone, in deep conversation, presumably about work. The crease of her forehead and the way she furiously scribbled notes told me she had more pressing matters at hand than accompanying me to check out mom's house.

"I'll call you in a bit," I whispered. "Keep working."

She smiled and nodded as I closed her bedroom door behind me. It seemed I would be facing the first day at the house on my own, which, truth be told, was probably for the best. I had no idea what I would find or how being in the house might affect me. Stella staying at the hotel was a good idea.

I grabbed my purse and locked the hotel room door behind me, then hopped into the elevator and walked quickly to the parking lot. Jumping in my SUV, I tossed my purse on the passenger seat and turned the ignition. I was flipping through radio stations when I got the distinct sensation that someone was watching me. The hairs on the back of my neck began to prickle, and I felt someone's eyes on me. I glanced around the parking lot, but there was no one nearby. All the other cars in the lot were empty.

Chalking it up to stress, I put the car into Reverse, zoomed out of the lot, and headed east on Main Street. Looking around, it was as if I had been transported back in time. Cottage Brook was the town that time forgot. Literally nothing had changed since the last time I had been there.

Storefront windows held the same tired displays they had when I was a kid, and I wondered how the mom-and-pop shops managed to stay in business with online shopping and big box stores. At the end of Main, I turned right and sighed with relief when I saw that something new had been added after all. There, shining like a beacon in the night, was a cute little coffee drive-thru.

I pulled up to the barista and ordered a triple espresso. While she made my drink, I tried to ignore the knots tightening in my stomach. The task ahead was unpleasant, but that didn't matter. It still had to be done. She handed me the coffee, and I took a sip, closing my eyes as the hot liquid warmed my throat. It was delicious, and I made a mental note that the coffee shop should become part of my morning routine. I was both shocked and thankful that I'd found a good cup of coffee in the sleepy town of Cottage Brook.

Pulling away from the coffee shop, I hooked a right, and then made an immediate left onto Blackbird Lane. Swallowing hard, I surveyed the houses I'd seen every single day of my childhood. Most of them looked exactly the same, maybe a little worse for wear. I wondered if the people who lived inside were the same; not that I really knew any of them. My mom had forbidden close relationships with anyone outside our home. She didn't want people to discover the hell in which we lived.

I slowed the car and maneuvered it into the driveway, coming to a stop in front of my childhood house. Turning off the ignition, I took a deep breath and gave myself a silent pep talk. When I gained my courage, I stepped outside, closing the door quietly so as not to awaken the ghosts inside the house.

My feet crunched in the gravel, which had been mostly overtaken by weeds. The house, once painted an ironic sunny yellow, was faded and peeling. The navy-blue shutters were cracked, and the one next to the large bay window in front was hanging haphazardly on its hinges. It looked like a slight breeze would send it crashing to the ground below.

The grass was nearly as tall as my waist, and the shrubbery in front of the house was feral and overgrown. The gutter swayed in the wind, threatening to fall on my head as I approached the front door.

Stooping down, I lifted the filthy welcome mat and grabbed the key that was still hidden underneath. My mother was nothing if not predictable. Twisting the knob, I opened the door, gasping as the smell of my childhood assaulted my senses. It was a noxious combination of filth and stale beer, and I felt familiar tears sting my eyes.

Walking through the house, I tried looking at things with an impartial eye, doing my best to push my emotions aside and simply take stock of what needed to be done. Every surface of the place needed a thorough cleaning, and it would take several truckloads to rid the house of all the junk and clutter. The walls needed to be patched and repainted, the old carpet had to be torn up and replaced, and several of the ceilings had water stains, indicating leaks. I had no idea how extensive the structural damage was, but it was all quite overwhelming.

Venturing into the kitchen, I wrinkled my nose at the shabby, ripped linoleum. The sight of it was enough to make me nauseous. I had spent far too much time curled up on that floor, cowering in fear as my mother searched the kitchen for implements intended to mete out punishments for my shortcomings, both real and imagined.

"I said you don't deserve dinner tonight after what you've done," my mother screamed, veins bulging at her temples.

"But I'm hungry. You took away my dinner yesterday too," I cried, my stomach growling so loud I was certain she could hear it.

"Maybe you'll learn if you go hungry long enough."

She bent down and stuck her face within an inch of mine, the anger rolling off her body like waves.

"I don't even know what I did wrong," I whimpered.

Before the words were out of my mouth, my moth-

er's hand flew into the air, smacking me across the face.

Back in the present, my head jerked in response and my hand flew to my cheek. The memory was so vivid I could almost feel her slap.

"Don't go there, Hadley," I said through gritted teeth, my voice echoing in the empty room. "Just don't go there. Turn it off. Pack it up. Shut it down."

Looking for a distraction, I opened the refrigerator door, finding it empty except for a single can of beer. The only thing surprising about that discovery was the fact that it was there. I was shocked my mother hadn't guzzled it the minute it hit her hands. She'd never shown any restraint when it came to alcohol.

"You're a worthless girl. I swear, you'll never make anything of yourself!"

My mother staggered across the kitchen floor, almost falling on her face as she grabbed the table to keep from toppling over. I sat in the chair, cringing in fear as she approached me. Nothing good ever came from being in such close proximity to my mother. She leaned down to me, and the smell of beer caused my stomach to turn. I hated her and everything about her.

My head swam, and my heart pounded. My breath came fast and hard, and I knew I was on the verge of a full-blown panic attack. Slamming the refrigerator door, I walked over to the kitchen table, which seemed to be the only thing in the house that wasn't filled with junk and clutter. Sinking into one of the rickety chairs, I buried my face in my hands and talked myself off the proverbial ledge.

I pushed down the memories that swam to the surface. If I allowed myself to go under too far, I would surely drown. I closed my eyes tightly and counted backwards from one hundred, taking deep, steadying breaths with each count. By the time I hit fifty, my breathing wasn't so ragged. By the time I got to one, I no longer felt like I was going to vomit. I opened my eyes and looked around the kitchen. The sooner I got to work, the sooner I could rid myself of the nightmare house. In order to do that, I had to make a game plan.

Honestly, I had no idea where to start. So many things needed to be done; the house was in shambles. Most of the work was far beyond the scope of my abilities. I could paint, clean, and decorate, but I had never been skilled at manual labor. I certainly wasn't qualified to do extensive home repairs and remodeling. That was going to require an actual contractor, which was also going to require money.

The thought of money caused my stomach to

knot even tighter, seeing as I had none. As an attorney, Charlie was financially set, and we had lived
quite comfortably. We always had what we needed
and most of what we wanted. I left the financial decisions to him, as they held little interest for me. He
created our budget and took care of money matters,
and that had always been just fine with me.

I'd assumed we were in a good place. I'd assumed
we had adequate life insurance. I'd assumed—if I
were to ever find myself in an unfortunate situation
like my current one—that Charlie would have had
the foresight to make sure my future was secure. I'd
since learned that assumptions were dangerous
things to make. When it all fell apart, I was left
picking up the pieces, free falling with no safety net.
To my utter dismay, after his death, I discovered that
Charlie had a few secrets of his own.

As my husband's hidden life surfaced, I began to
wonder if I had ever really known him at all. The
steady, responsible man I'd fallen in love with
seemed to be a distant memory. I always believed
Charlie would do anything to take care of his family,
but the more I discovered about him, the less faith I
had in my belief. My husband felt like a stranger
to me.

Not only had Charlie allowed our life insurance policy to lapse, he'd also had a gambling problem he kept so far under wraps that I only found out about it once he was dead. He had spent all of our money, including any savings we ever had, on his gambling debts. As if that wasn't bad enough, he had also taken out second and third mortgages on our home. With Charlie gone, I was so far in the hole financially that I doubted I would ever find my way out. These revelations had me second-guessing everything. Since his death, I'd started wondering what else I hadn't known about my husband.

The only thing keeping me afloat was the wad of cash I'd found hidden in Charlie's sock drawer. I had no idea why it was there, or what he'd intended to do with it, but it was keeping me alive, and that's all that mattered to me. As I thought of all the work that needed to be done on my mother's house, a growing feeling of desperation began to take over. I needed to sell the house, but no one was going to buy it the way it was, and I didn't have the funds available to remodel it. I had no idea what to do.

As I fiddled with the chipped paint on the kitchen table, I noticed an envelope lying there. Pulling it toward me, I was surprised to find my name written across the front. Curious, I ripped it open. Inside was a note. When I unfolded the paper, a credit card clattered onto the tabletop.

Dear Hadley,

I knew if I gave this to you at my house, you would have found some way to refuse it. Now that you've seen the state of your mother's home, you know as well as I do the cost involved to fix it. I know you're not in a position right now to afford to do so, and I'm an old woman who has nothing better to do with all of my money.

This credit card is yours, and it has no spending limit. Use it for repairs, for paying a contractor, and for getting yourself back on your feet. Use it for whatever you need—but please use it. I don't want to hear a word about it. I've always loved you as if you were my own daughter. It's time you let me help you.

Aunt Viv

"How does she always manage to do exactly the right thing at exactly the right moment?" I muttered to myself. "I want to be just like her when I grow up."

I took my wallet from my purse, nestling the credit card safely inside. I wiped the stream of tears from my eyes as a tiny bit of the weight lifted off of my shoulders. As much as I hated to accept help, I knew that piece of plastic was my lifeline, and Aunt

Viv was surely my guardian angel. Thanks to her, I would be able to remodel my dump of a childhood home and sell it. Seeing as it had been paid off years ago, I would actually stand to make a profit. Maybe things were looking up after all.

I continued walking through the rest of the house, scribbling notes of the work that needed to be done. Finishing up the torturous home tour, I decided I'd had enough for the day. I wanted to go back to the hotel and make a giant to-do list. Making lists was the way I kept my racing thoughts organized. It gave me a modicum of control. I needed to find a landscaper and a contractor, ones who weren't afraid of a mountain of work. I had no idea where to look, but I was pretty good with Google.

Locking the door behind me, I walked to my car. Slipping into the driver seat, I glanced at the house next door to my mother's, which I hadn't paid much attention to earlier. It was by far the nicest one on the street, and whoever renovated it had clearly known what they were doing. I remembered the house always having good bones, but the last time I had seen it, it was in desperate need of a face-lift. Someone clearly gave it one.

I noticed a large truck sitting in the driveway and saw the decal on the side, which read Kinley Home

Remodeling. Grabbing a pen and piece of paper, I jotted down the phone number written on the side of the truck.

What a stroke of luck! I wasn't a huge believer in coincidences, but I had always been sure that everything happened for a reason. Perhaps the remodeled house next door and the contractor's truck were signs. If Kinley Home Remodeling had worked on the neighbor's house, that was a good enough reference for me. Maybe I'd found my new contractor already.

CHAPTER EIGHT

THE NEXT MORNING, I GRABBED MY TRIPLE espresso at the same little coffee shop. Stella was tied up again with work, but promised she'd come and help as soon as she could. I knew she felt guilty, but I assured her she was doing exactly what she needed to be doing—focusing on her business and her future.

I headed back to my mother's house, feeling more organized than I had in weeks. I was lighter and, dare I say, even a little optimistic. It seemed that things had finally turned a corner, and maybe I was going to be all right after all.

I'd spent the rest of yesterday contacting landscapers. One was recommended by the hotel manager, and the other was the landscaper Aunt Viv had always used. I'd met them both at my mother's house, walked them through the jungle of her yard, and settled on the one Aunt Viv recommended. He had given the lowest bid, but he also seemed the most knowledgeable. He'd worked for Viv for several years, and she'd always been pleased with his work. I trusted Viv's opinion of people implicitly.

The landscaper had put me on his schedule and planned to send out a crew to get started that morning. He told me the decorative landscaping would have to wait until after the home renovations, but he was willing to tear out shrubs and get the grass and weeds under control right away. I was surprised and grateful that he was moving on it so quickly, as I was more than a little afraid of what rodents might be lurking under all that lawn debris. I admired his promptness and felt even better about my choice.

I'd also called the number for Kinley Home Remodeling that I'd seen on the truck next door. I'd left a message, and the receptionist had called me back, saying that Mr. Kinley could meet me that morning at my mother's address if I wanted an estimate. I'd scheduled the appointment and written it into the planner I'd purchased the day before. I was anxious to get started, because the sooner the work began, the sooner I could sell the place and be rid of it forever.

Pulling into the driveway, I was pleased to see the landscaping crew was already there, hard at work. Two men were removing a large section of the shrubbery in front of the bay window, opening things up to let the light in. Another worker was tackling the out-of-control lawn, mowing it into submission. Things were in motion, and it felt good. I was in control of my life for the first time in a long time.

I glanced at the house next door, surprised to see that the truck from Kinley Home Remodeling was parked there once again. I wondered why the vehicle was there and not at my mother's house. Looking at my watch, I saw it was only a few minutes until my appointment time. Shrugging, I stepped out of the car and headed inside the house. If Kinley Home Remodeling was a large business, they probably had lots of company trucks.

Grabbing a trash bag, I decided I would begin the daunting cleanup process inside while I waited. I started tossing junk that was piled up in the living room, busying myself until the contractor arrived. I had nearly filled the bag to the top when I heard a knock at the front door. Tying a knot in it, I dropped it on the floor and went to answer.

Had I known what was about to happen, I might have taken an extra second to compose myself. But I couldn't have known. There's no way I could have been prepared. Never in my wildest dreams would I have imagined what awaited me on the other side of that door.

Twisting the knob, I swung open the door, my jaw nearly hitting the floor when I saw who was standing there. It was a total gut punch, seeing him again. His scent, the one that had haunted me for over a year, wafted through the air, giving me an immediate head rush. It was the smell of citrus and cedar, the smell of longing and confusion, the smell of everything terrible and unexpected that had brought me to the lowest point in my life.

One hand flew to my mouth in a futile attempt to stifle the gasp that escaped unbidden from my lips. The other hand gripped the door frame to steady legs that had suddenly been rendered useless. Heart pounding, head swimming, ears ringing, I opened my mouth to speak, but nothing came out.

His reaction was quite different than mine. His face broke out into the widest, most dazzling, genuine smile I had ever seen.

He spoke, and at the same moment, I also found my voice.

"It's you," we stated in unison.

CHAPTER NINE

TAKING A STEP BACKWARD, I STUMBLED. Reacting quickly, he stepped inside, reaching out to grab my arm, steadying me and making me dizzy all at the same time. The heat of his hand caused my entire body to tingle, and I wasn't sure if I liked the feeling or not. All I knew for certain was that everything about the situation and his close proximity shook me to my very core.

I took another step backwards, needing to put some space between us. I pulled my arm away quickly, covering the spot where his hand had been as if it were an open wound. I knew my mouth was gaping wide, but I couldn't seem to close it. I couldn't do much of anything but stare into the intoxicating blue eyes of the man I'd met in the coffee shop the year before.

"It—It's you—" I stammered in disbelief.

"It's me. And I guess we've established that it's you," he chuckled, seemingly adjusting to the shock much better than I.

The sound of his laugh took me back to that day, sitting across from him at the table. His laughter was like music. I remembered I kept trying to find silly things to say, just so I could hear him laugh.

"I—I don't—understand," I offered weakly as I shook my head from side to side.

"I'm the contractor," he shrugged.

"You're Mr. Kinley?"

"Guilty as charged." He smiled. "Mack Kinley, owner of Kinley Home Remodeling."

"Your name is Mack."

It wasn't a question. It was more a moment of clarity. For over a year I had wondered what his name was. I'd imagined every possibility under the sun, wishing I knew. I had laid my heart bare before him that day, yet never actually introduced myself. He hadn't either. Our souls had recognized each other, and names had seemed unimportant. I'd spilled my guts to a nameless man, and nothing had ever felt more right. Now, it felt strange for him to know so much about me, yet I had just found out his name.

"Yes, my name is Mack," he confirmed with a smile, his dimple peeking out. "And yours is Hadley Monroe."

"Yes," I answered, still shaking my head as if trying to stop his words from gaining purchase.

"Hadley. The name suits you. I've wondered about it for a long time," Mack said wistfully, his eyes searching mine.

"You have?" I swallowed hard, caught up in the moment. Then I remembered what was happening and I continued with, "This is ridiculous."

"It's something, that's for sure. Although ridiculous isn't really the word I would choose."

A jolt of anger shot through me. It was unexpected and sudden, and I didn't know where it came from or why it was there. But it was, and I wasn't capable of doing anything besides reacting to it.

"Oh yeah? Well, exactly what word would *you* choose, Mack Kinley?" I snapped; a ball of rage was ready to erupt inside my belly.

"Unexpected. Serendipitous. Fate."

"That's three words," I spat, my cheeks beginning to burn.

"So it is," he agreed jovially, seemingly unaffected by my reaction.

Not knowing what else to say, I stood there stewing in my fury. Mack, finally taking a minute to read the room, stepped back and scrutinized me closely.

"Hadley, I'm getting the feeling that you're angry with me for some reason, but I'm not sure why."

"This! You!" I gestured awkwardly, my arms flailing about haphazardly. "Why are you here?" My head spun dizzyingly, my heart pounding like a bass drum inside my chest. I felt like I couldn't get a full breath. I knew it was unfair and unreasonable to unleash my wrath on him, but I couldn't seem to help myself.

"Well, Hadley, I'm here because you called and made an appointment with my receptionist," he answered evenly.

"But that was before I knew!"

"Knew what?"

"Before I knew that you were you," I exploded.

"I've always been me," he joked, his laugh suddenly grating on my frazzled nerves.

"This isn't funny!" I stormed, stomping my foot like a child throwing a temper tantrum.

"Okay, look," he began, trying to placate my foul

disposition. "I know this is a shock. It's a shock for me too. I thought I would never see you again after that day. But if I'm being honest, I'm not sorry to see you right now."

The burning, boiling feeling in my gut grew stronger, and I felt like I was literally going to explode. I couldn't let him see me like that. I was about to cross over the point of no return.

"You need to go," I demanded, pushing him toward the door.

"You don't want me to look at the house?"

"No, I don't want you to look at the house! Get out!" I screamed, knowing that in another second it would be too late.

"I'll go, but unfortunately, you're probably going to see me again," Mack replied calmly as he allowed me to hasten him out the door.

"And why would I ever have to see you again?"

"Because I live next door," he chuckled.

Before I could say another word or think of a good comeback or possibly throw something at him, Mack turned and walked away. With a growl, I slammed the door shut behind him.

CHAPTER TEN

IN A BIT OF A DAZE, I STOOD THERE, MY HAND ON the doorknob, trying to make sense of what had just happened. Turning slowly, I walked to the kitchen, which was still the only place clean enough for me to sit. Slumping into the chair, I exhaled the breath I had been holding. Never in a million years did I expect to see Mack Kinley, mystery man extraordinaire, standing at my mother's door.

I thought back to the day we met, remembering the warmth he'd radiated. I'd felt more comfortable with him than I had ever felt with anyone in my life. I'd told him things I had never told anyone, including far too much about my tumultuous and toxic relationship with my mother. Had I even had an inkling that the man might ever come across my mother, I would have kept my mouth shut about her. I specifically spilled my guts to him because I knew he had no clue who she was. Of all the places in the entire world for him to live, next door to her was the very definition of irony.

I tried to steady my nerves, to focus in on what I was actually feeling beneath the anger. Disentangling my emotions was a tough one for me. So much of my life had been spent hiding and masking my feelings, so tapping into them was difficult. I had seen a therapist for a few years during a particularly rough patch of my life, and she had worked with me to identify and recognize my feelings.

For most, that wasn't a particularly difficult task. If people grew up in an environment where they were allowed to freely express themselves, it tended to come naturally. If they were sad, they allowed themselves to be sad. If they were angry, they felt it.

That was the healthy way to deal with feelings and emotions. But that had never been the case for me.

Living in a home where my moods had to be altered based upon my mother's behavior stunted my emotional growth. I never had the luxury of actually feeling my feelings. I learned at a very early age that the only emotion I had permission to feel was guilt. I survived my traumatic and abusive past by being agreeable and never rocking the boat. My actual feelings were of little concern to anyone.

Unfortunately, my upbringing turned me into an adult who cared only about the health and well-being of others. What I wanted or needed never even factored into the equation. My childhood turned me into a woman who only knew how to be a people pleaser. I was someone who had no clue what I actually felt or what to do with those feelings when I experienced them.

Working with the therapist had opened my eyes in a lot of ways, and she had given me tools to help identify and manage my feelings. Most importantly, she taught me that when I felt overwhelmed, as I did in that moment, it was important to sit with my emotions and listen, to really try to zero in on exactly what I was feeling. Often my true emotions were masked by more easily accessible ones, like anger or guilt.

I sighed. It seemed that was what had happened with Mack. The shock and fear I felt upon seeing his face was immediately masked by anger. After reflecting for a few minutes, I understood that my anger wasn't directed toward Mack at all. He had done nothing wrong. I was angry with myself, angry with my situation. Mack had simply been on the receiving end of my misdirected ire.

Yes, I was surprised to see him. That may have been the understatement of the year. I went back to that coffee shop every single day for a month after I met him, just hoping to run into him again. I had wanted to see him more than anything. So, it seemed unlikely that seeing him again would cause me to be angry.

The anger probably stemmed from the fact that, only moments before, I had felt confident, optimistic, and in control for the first time in a very long while. Seeing Mack had blown me out of the water yet again. Knowing that he lived next door to my mother and was a potential contractor for remodeling her house left me feeling anything but stable and in control.

Taking it down another layer, beneath the anger, there was guilt—always the guilt.

The sight of Mack reminded me of how fixated I'd become on him after that day in the coffee shop. Meeting him had caused me to question everything, including my marriage to Charlie. I had thought of Mack incessantly, fantasized about him to the point that it distracted me from everything else in my life, especially Charlie.

Most of all, the fact that I couldn't eradicate the memory of Mack eventually led to me making the insane announcement that I was having an affair that never actually happened. My fascination with Mack led me to say the words that killed my husband. Thus, the guilt.

When I laid it all out, piece by piece, I realized anger wasn't the emotion I was actually feeling. It was fear. It was grief. It was guilt. It had all mixed together to form a terrible stew inside me, and when I saw Mack, it spewed out as anger, one of the most easily accessible emotions. I owed Mack a very large apology.

Steeling myself for what I had to do, I headed toward the front door. I stepped outside and rounded the corner of the garage, where, to my surprise, Mack was standing. He was leaning against the garage door, calmly watching the landscapers pull the shrubs.

"These guys are good. I use them on a lot of my jobs," he said casually, not making eye contact with me.

"My aunt recommended them," I answered quietly, the guilt and humiliation pressing down on me a little bit more.

Mack had every right to be furious with me,

given the way I had treated him. He hadn't deserved to be yelled at or shoved out the door. I would have understood if he wanted to return the favor and lash out at me too. But looking at him as he leaned against my mother's garage, I noticed that he appeared to be anything but angry. He looked calm and unruffled.

"Look, I need to apologize," I began, my cheeks flushing with embarrassment as I thought about my behavior.

"Accepted," he said with a grin, keeping his eyes on the ground.

"But I haven't done it yet."

"You don't need to." He shrugged.

"But I do," I insisted.

"No, you don't."

"But actually, I do," I argued.

"Are you going to yell at me again?" He turned those twinkling blue eyes on me, undoing me completely, making my insides turn to mush. "I mean, it's fine if you want to yell, but I'd like to brace myself first." He grinned widely, the dimple in his cheek deepening.

I laughed wryly and shook my head. "No, I'm not going to yell at you again. At least not right now."

"Good. You're terrifying when you're angry." He widened his eyes in mock fear.

"Like I said, I want to apologize. I was way out of line, and there are no excuses for my behavior. But I was just so... shocked... to see you. I reacted badly."

"It was pretty surprising, huh? I thought I would never see you again after that day," Mack agreed.

"Same here," I answered.

"I mean, I was just passing through Cleveland, happened to go into a coffee shop I'd never been in before, met this incredible woman, and had one of the best conversations of my life," he recounted.

"Yeah, that day was unexpected," I agreed.

My heart was nearly bursting to hear that our encounter had meant something to him too. I mean, I knew it had, but hearing him say the words was just the confirmation I needed. It hadn't been one-sided.

"So... are you going to let me inside to look at your mother's house?"

"Look at her house?"

"Well, yeah, it will be easier to give you an accurate bid if I've actually seen it."

He stuffed his hands into the pockets of his jeans and shifted awkwardly from foot to foot.

"You mean you still want to do it? Even after I yelled at you?"

"I have wanted to get my hands on this place ever since I moved in next door five years ago. The structure of the house is just wonderful, and I have so many plans and ideas to really bring out its best features."

"Plus the commute isn't too bad," I joked.

"Not too bad at all."

"If you're sure..." I hesitated.

"There's a lot of potential here," he said quietly.

I realized that he wasn't looking at the house anymore. He was looking at me.

"It needs a lot of work, Mack," I replied, not quite sure if I was talking about myself or the house.

"I've never been afraid of hard work. The toughest things tend to be the most rewarding. I would love to have the job."

I glanced up at the peeling paint and broken shutters. When I looked at the house on 1223 Blackbird Lane, I saw nothing but sadness and decay. It was impossible for me to see what Mack saw. But I liked that he was a man with a vision, and if he could turn the dump into something decent instead of the monstrous eyesore it was, maybe he was the right man for the job.

"All right, Mack Kinley. If you're sure you want to take this on, let's go inside."

CHAPTER ELEVEN

I FOLLOWED MACK THROUGH MY MOTHER'S
house as he observed every dilapidated nook and
cranny. It was difficult for me to spend so much time
walking through my childhood home, but Mack kept
up a steady stream of conversation, which served as a
good distraction from the horrific memories that tried
to surface in each room. Not to mention the fact that,
once I had relaxed into the situation, being near him
was just as easy as it had been that day in the coffee
shop.

"So, what are your plans for the place?" Mack
stooped down and lifted a corner of worn-out shag
carpeting. "Will you be living here?"

"No, definitely not. I'll be selling it," I replied

without a second's hesitation. "As soon as humanly possible."

"You'll get a good price for it after I'm finished," he replied with a grin as he stood to face me.

His dimpled smile caused my stomach to turn triple somersaults. He elicited an unprecedented physical response in me, and I wasn't quite sure what to do about it. I was in very far over my head, and the water kept getting deeper.

"That's great," I said as I cleared my throat, which had suddenly gone as dry as sandpaper. "I'm counting on a good sale price."

"Your mother doesn't want to live here anymore?" He pulled open a door leading to the storage space in the wall and stuck his head inside.

"She—uh—she can't—I mean—she won't—" I stammered, not sure what to say.

"Oh, Hadley, I'm sorry. That was rude of me to stick my nose in where it doesn't belong. It's none of my business," he apologized.

"It's okay. Really. It's just that it's all very new information for me. I'm still trying to wrap my head around what happened to her."

"I gathered something was wrong when they took her off in an ambulance a few weeks ago. I never saw her come back," he answered as he closed the crawl space door.

"She won't be coming back," I said quietly.

"Did she....?" Mack's words trailed off.

"No, she's still alive. But they say she doesn't have much time left."

"I'm sorry, Hadley. I didn't know. Your mother kept to herself, and she made it clear she liked things that way."

"She's a real gem," I replied sarcastically.

"If you don't mind me asking, what's wrong with her?"

"She has dementia, which I just found out about recently. The funny thing is that she's apparently had it for years and I never knew. So, sign me up for Daughter of the Year, I suppose."

"It sounds like you're blaming yourself for not knowing. Am I right?" Mack said casually.

"She's my mother. I should have known."

"I seem to recall you had a pretty toxic relationship with your mom. The things you told me she did to you, Hadley, well, I think you made the only choice possible in distancing yourself from her."

"You remember what I told you about my mom?"

"I remember every single word you said that day," Mack answered, his eyes locking onto mine.

"Me too," I whispered, caught up in his spell.

We stared at each other for a couple of seconds without speaking. I had no idea how he could consume me so quickly and completely, but he did. I needed to rein it in. I couldn't let this—whatever it was—happen. My inability to keep my head on straight around Mack was dangerous. I wasn't in the right frame of mind to take on anything else. As wonderful as Mack was, nothing could happen between us. I needed to remember that.

Mack was there to fix my mother's house. Nothing more. Nothing less.

I broke eye contact and continued walking. He followed, and I could feel the tension between us, lingering in the air like perfume. My thoughts were running a mile a minute, and all I wanted to do was tell him how I really felt, but I knew better. Once I opened that door, it couldn't be closed.

We made our way through the entire house as Mack scribbled notes onto his clipboard.

"So, what's the damage going to be?" I asked nervously as we sat at the kitchen table.

Mack scribbled something else onto a sheet of paper, folded it, and slid it across the table toward me.

"Here's the breakdown and estimate. It's probably best if you look at that later." He smiled, drumming his fingers on the tabletop.

"That bad, huh?" I rolled my eyes and stuffed the paper into the pocket of my jeans.

"Well, the house needs a lot of work. And I'm the best around."

"And so modest too!" I tried for a joke, hoping it would lighten the mood. Leaning back in the chair, I folded my arms.

"So—uh—there's something I want to ask, but I don't want to seem too forward," Mack began,

clearing his throat nervously.

"Go ahead. You already know more about me than most people," I replied with a shrug, more than a little worried about what he was going to say.

"When we met that day, you talked about your husband. From what you told me, it sounded like you two were going through a bit of a rough patch," he said as he met my eyes. "Can I ask what happened? Did you work things out?"

I took a deep breath and considered his question. How was I supposed to answer it? How would Mack feel if I told him the truth—that Charlie was dead and I was still struggling with guilt because I had confessed to an affair I never had with Mack, and

Charlie had died believing the lie? Too much to reveal? Probably.

"Well, my husband passed away about six months ago," I answered, cushioning the truth.

"Oh wow. Oh, Hadley, I'm so sorry. I shouldn't have asked. It's really none of my business," Mack apologized profusely, awkwardly wiping his palms on the fabric of his jeans.

"It was a legitimate question, given our conversation that day," I replied, uncrossing my arms and placing my hands on the table.

"I had no idea. I mean, I thought maybe you might have separated or divorced, or maybe you'd gone the therapy route instead, but I wouldn't have dreamed that he had died. And so recently," Mack rambled. "How are you? I mean, that's a stupid question, isn't it? I'm so sorry, I—"

"Mack," I interrupted. "It's okay. I'm fine. Really. I'm all right. Or as all right as I can be."

"You really do have a lot on your plate, don't you? Between your mom and your husband. How are your daughters holding up?"

"They're hanging in there," I replied, caught off guard by the fact that he remembered me talking about my daughters.

"What can I do? How can I help you?"

He swiped his hands through his hair quickly, clearly not sure what to do with them, then reached across the table, gently placing them on top of mine. The compassion in his eyes broke me.

I felt caught up in a waterfall of emotion, the circumstances of the past few months finally pulling me under. The warmth and sincerity on Mack's face drew me in, wrapping around me like a warm embrace. My lip quivered, and my eyes filled with tears, and no matter how hard I tried to steel myself, it was no use. It seemed that I could hide my feelings around everyone—except for Mack Kinley.

As soon as the first teardrop fell, it was only a matter of time before the deluge.

"Hey, it's okay, come here," Mack whispered, rising from his chair.

He stood in front of me as I sat in the chair. He leaned down and pulled me close, wrapping his strong arms around my shaking body. It should have been awkward, given the fact that my face was buried somewhere in his middle, but it wasn't. In fact, nothing had ever felt more right.

Somewhere in the back of my mind a voice was screaming at me to push him away. I heard it, yelling faintly in the background, but I didn't listen. Instead,

I felt myself sink farther into his embrace, melting like butter in his arms.

Mack was everything strong and steady that I had needed the past several months. I had been so strong, never caving in for a second. I had kept my composure, thinking only of my daughters' needs and all that had to be done. I had forced myself to put one foot in front of the other every single day, moving forward perpetually, doing everything I was supposed to do.

But I hadn't allowed myself to wallow, to grieve. I hadn't allowed myself to be comforted.

In that moment, I forgot about everything and everyone and let the tears fall. I cried for all I had lost. I let the grief wash over me, and I felt it. For the first time in as long as I could remember, I was fully present in the moment, feeling my true feelings. Mack just held me, stroking his hands across my back in a strangely calming rhythm. It felt good, and it felt right. Desire stirred inside me, taking my breath away with its intensity. I didn't even try to push it aside.

Magnetized, my body pulled toward his by sheer force, I stood and wrapped my arms around his neck. I looked into his eyes for a split second, drowning. Forgetting everything except how his body felt next to mine, I stood on my toes, pulling his face toward me. Sparks flew as his mouth consumed mine, taking me in, devouring me. Kissing Mack Kinley was everything I had ever imagined it would be. I never wanted it to stop.

But then I remembered the man who was holding me, and the grief receded as the guilt took over. I had no right to be kissed by him. Things were racing out of control, and I needed to put on the brakes before anything else happened.

Pulling away quickly, I wiped my tear-streaked eyes on the sleeve of my shirt. "Thank you for trying to comfort me, Mack, but I'm fine."

"There's no way you're fine, Hadley. And we should talk about what just happened. You don't have to be strong around me, you know," he replied, leaning toward me again.

I put my hands out to stop him. "I'm fine. Really. And I need to go. I forgot I have another appointment."

"Hadley—"

"I'll—uh—take a look at the estimate, but I'm sure it's great. How soon can you start?"

"Back to business, huh? All right then, we'll play it your way." Mack shook his head. "I—uh—can probably start in a couple of weeks. I just need to take a look at my schedule."

"Perfect. The sooner the better. I need to get rid of this place and move on with my life."

I swallowed hard as I grabbed my purse and headed out the front door, leaving him little choice but to follow me. Locking the door behind me, I walked quickly toward my car. Reaching inside, I grabbed a scrap of paper and jotted down my phone number.

"Here's my contact information. I'll wait to hear from you about when you can start."

Confusion played on Mack's face as he shoved the paper into his pocket. "Hadley—"

"Look, Mack, I appreciate your concern for me, but I'm fine. And we need to keep things professional. Nothing like that will be happening again."

"Professional? I think we're way past professional, Hadley," he insisted. "And if you would let your guard down for a minute, you'd be forced to admit that."

"Well, that's not going to happen," I said quickly.

"But Hadley—"

"Look, I've got a lot going on in my life right now, Mack. This is the best I can do. You're my contractor. That's all."

My heart actually hurt as I said the brutal words, but that's the way it needed to be.

"If you really feel that way..." Mack's face registered hurt and confusion.

"I do. I really do. Let me know when you can start on the house."

I smiled tightly and got into the car. Starting it up, I backed out of the driveway without looking at him. Yes, I was being harsh, but I had to be. The connection between us was undeniable. It was a lit match that I had to extinguish before things got out of control. I already had enough wildfires to put out.

Charlie's death still weighed on my conscience. I couldn't get past the fact that he had died without ever knowing the truth, and I didn't know if I ever would. I was too tangled up in my last relationship to jump into a new one. As much as I wanted things to be different, happiness just didn't seem to be in the cards for me.

CHAPTER TWELVE

AFTER LEAVING THE HOUSE, I DROVE AROUND aimlessly for the next hour. I didn't know how to process everything that had been thrown at me. I was glad to have found Mack, and I was excited to see what he was going to do with my mother's house, but the very idea of him complicated an already over-complicated situation. And I had kissed him. How was I supposed to keep things professional when everything inside me screamed otherwise? I didn't even know if professionalism was possible.

The only thing I was absolutely certain of was this—I could not become involved with Mack in any other way.

No matter how much I felt at home with him, no matter how perfectly we seemed to fit together, I couldn't even entertain the idea. Charlie was dead because of an accident resulting from our stupid argument. I never got the chance to make things right. My husband didn't get the chance to be happy, so it seemed fitting that I shouldn't either.

A new relationship was off the table for me. Besides, I had far more important things to figure out. I needed to focus on deciding what to do with the rest of my life. I had to find a source of income. I couldn't live off Aunt Viv's credit card and Charlie's wad of mystery cash forever.

I had no real employment experience to speak of. The only job I'd ever had was at the law firm where I'd met Charlie, and that hadn't lasted long enough to really count. I had few marketable skills, and the only talent I had was artistic. Creative skills weren't notorious for being big money makers.

Besides the financial burden, I needed to fix up my mother's house and sell it. I needed to make sure my daughters were happy and healthy, moving on in a life in which their father wasn't present. And I needed to come to terms with the fact that my mother was going to die and I had no idea how I felt about it. My world had imploded, and I was left holding the pieces.

Mack Kinley and his intuitive, compassionate,

all-seeing blue eyes, and insanely kissable lips couldn't even factor into the equation of my messed-up life.

My stomach growled loudly, and I realized I was hungry. I pulled into the closest drive-thru, Foodie Land, and grabbed a burger, fries, and a milkshake, reminding myself that I would eat healthier tomorrow. I maneuvered the car into the parking lot of the fast-food joint and began stuffing the burger into my mouth and guzzling the shake, thankful no one could see me. I felt like I had sunk to an all-time low.

I must have crammed in too much at once, because a chunk of the burger got stuck and I began to cough, frantically slurping on the milkshake in an effort to wash it down. My eyes were watering, my nose was running, and my throat felt like it was on fire. I coughed again, clearing my airway and sucking down another drink of the milkshake to soothe it.

I caught a glimpse of myself in the rearview mirror—red eyes, runny nose, mascara streaks trailing down my face—and I began to laugh. At first it began as a chuckle, but at some point it bubbled into a full belly laugh. My emotions were raw and close to the surface, though, and the laughter quickly turned to tears, which soon led to full body-racking sobs.

I sat in the parking lot and cried so hard I could

barely breathe. Was I having a nervous breakdown? Maybe I needed to call my therapist and beg her to counsel me right then and there. Either way, I needed to get my act together. I didn't want to be taken out by choking on fast food in the middle of an out-of-control crying jag.

I could almost see the headline: *Middle-Aged Mother Chokes To Death On Burger While Questioning Her Life Decisions in Foodie Land Parking Lot.*

"Pull yourself together, woman," I commanded myself.

Wiping my face, I tossed my trash into the empty food bag and threw it on the floor. I had just managed to get my tears under control when my phone rang. Glancing at the display, I saw that it was Celeste.

I took a deep breath, put a smile on my face, and answered, "Hey, baby."

"Hi, Mom. How are you doing?"

"Great!" I said, probably too brightly.

"Are you sure? You don't sound great. You sound fake happy." My oldest daughter was like her father, the skeptical one.

"I'm doing really well, honey. I just met with the contractor at Grandma's house. The landscapers are getting the yard in shape, and I feel like I have a good solid plan," I lied, working to make my voice sound chipper, but not "fake happy."

"That's good. You aren't wasting any time, are you?" Celeste chuckled.

"I want to get it sold as soon as possible," I answered. "I need to put that part of my life behind me."

"Good riddance to bad rubbish, or something like that?" she asked with a laugh.

"Exactly. How are things there? How's work?"

I changed the subject, knowing it was safest to keep her talking about herself so she didn't ask questions I didn't want to answer.

"Work is good. My job is interesting. I actually really like it," Celeste replied. "But I miss you and Stella. And I feel bad that I'm not there to help."

"You're exactly where you're supposed to be, baby. You're making a life for yourself. You're securing your future. That's all I have ever wanted for you and your sister."

"How's Stella? I tried to call her earlier, but she didn't answer."

"She's good. She was busy with work when I left this morning, so she stayed behind at the hotel."

"Hotel? You're not staying at Grandma's house?"

"No, we're not. Aunt Viv put us up in the Lexington Hotel," I answered.

"The Lexington? I think I remember it. It looks like a castle, right?"

"Yep, that's the place. Grandma's house wasn't really fit to live in, so Aunt Viv rented out the Presidential Suite for us."

"Fancy schmancy, Mom. That's pretty cool of her."

"Aunt Viv is great. She can't wait to meet you," I replied.

"It's so weird that I've never met my own aunt," Celeste stated.

"Our family is beyond weird, honey." I rolled my eyes.

"That's the truth. Hey, I just found out that have a long weekend coming up at the end of the month. I thought I would drive down to see you guys."

"We would love that," I answered happily. "I miss you."

"I miss you too. I think this is the longest I've gone without seeing you in my whole life."

"You're probably right, come to think of it," I answered.

"Everyone I know went away to college, but I

was always glad I lived at home and commuted to school." Celeste laughed. "Crazy, huh?"

"I've never liked being away from you girls."

"My friends are all jealous that I have such a good relationship with my mom. They say they wish they could talk to their moms like I talk to you."

"Well, then I've done something right, I suppose. A good relationship with you girls was my top priority."

"You're the best," Celeste answered. "I've got to run, Mom. My break is over. I'll call you tomorrow."

"Talk to you soon. Love you, honey."

"Love you too, Mom."

I smiled as I hung up the phone. My life might be a total dumpster fire on all sides, but I knew I had done at least one thing right—I was a great mom, and no one could convince me otherwise.

Then a nagging thought crept into my brain, unpacked its bags, and took up residence. Would my daughters still feel the same way about me if they knew the truth? Would they look at me differently if they knew the last words I ever spoke to their father were the very ones that caused him to get into that car?

CHAPTER THIRTEEN

Two more weeks passed, and it seemed like my life was finally settling into a steady, albeit stressful, rhythm. Mack's goal was to start working at my mom's house the following week, and I was getting antsy waiting for him to begin. He was finishing up a job that was taking much longer than planned, or at least that's what he told me. A part of me worried that he was avoiding me on purpose, which, truth be told, I couldn't really blame him for. I reminded myself to be patient, but I was having a difficult time with that. I hadn't seen Mack since that fateful day at my mother's house when I'd thrown myself at him. But if I was being honest, he was never far from my thoughts.

My days were spent job hunting, which had

amounted to a whole lot of nothing. Any jobs that were available required qualifications that I didn't have. Short of flipping burgers at Foodie Land, I was beginning to think I was basically unemployable.

Besides the disastrous job search, I was also trying to climb out from under the mountain of financial paperwork I had to deal with, as well as being forced to make uncomfortable decisions about selling my house in Cleveland.

Earlier that day, I'd had lunch with Aunt Viv, who had given me an update on my mother. According to her, Charlotte's health was rapidly declining, and her doctors didn't think she had much time left. I hadn't gone back to see her since the day I'd arrived in Cottage Brook, and I didn't know if I ever would. I kept waiting for the urge to kick in, but so far it hadn't. Strangely enough, I didn't feel quite as guilty about my lack of visits with my mom. For the first time in a long time, I was really trying to pay attention to my emotions surrounding my past with her.

I was learning to be in tune with myself, and I wasn't beating myself up about not wanting to see her. In fact, I was allowing myself to feel whatever it was that I felt at any given moment. Granting myself that permission was freeing. Unlike the way I'd dealt with her in the past—making myself hold on when I should really let go—I wasn't trying to force anything when it came to my mother. I was finally accepting our relationship, or lack thereof, and recognizing that some things might be too far gone to fix.

That evening, after a particularly stressful day, I was lying on the hotel couch aimlessly flipping through the channels. Earlier that afternoon I had crunched the numbers for my monthly budget, and my financial situation was even more dire than I'd previously understood. I was beyond broke. In order to divert my attention, I decided to numb myself with mindless reality television.

Stella had been locked in her room all afternoon, presumably tied up with work. Around seven o'clock, she finally emerged with a huge smile on her face.

"Wow, you've been at it for a while. You've had a long day."

I looked away from the television and sat up, patting the cushion beside me. Taking the hint, Stella flopped down beside me.

"It was a long day, but it was great. I have the best news," Stella gushed.

"What is it?"

"A huge retail store wants to carry my jewelry

line. Can you believe it?" She squealed loudly and clapped her hands with glee.

"Sweetie, that's fantastic!" I grabbed her, hugging her tightly. "That's what you've been working toward since you started."

"I know! I didn't think it would happen so soon. Apparently, the buyer for the store saw my jewelry online and fell in love with it. I've been on the phone most of the day making the deal," Stella explained excitedly.

"I am so proud of you. This deserves a celebration. Let's pick a restaurant and go out to dinner," I suggested. "My treat."

"Mom, I know you can't afford luxuries right now," Stella hedged.

"Tonight we're not worrying about my money, or lack thereof. I've got this covered. Go put on something fun and cute, and I'll do the same. Meet me back here in thirty minutes," I commanded.

With a thousand-watt smile, Stella nodded and ran to her room to change. I silently thanked Aunt Viv for the gift of the credit card and headed to my own room. Yes, money was tight, but some things still deserved to be celebrated, and Stella's news was one of them.

Rifling through the closet, I wrinkled up my nose

at my limited clothing selection. I tended to be a jeans and sweatshirt kind of woman, and most of the time, I opted for comfort over style. I didn't get dressed up too often, so my choices weren't as plentiful as I would have liked at that particular moment. I pulled out a green maxi-dress that I had worn the year before to an event Charlie and I had attended. I hadn't worn it since then, and had packed it on a whim in case I needed to get dressed up, but I was pretty sure it would still fit.

Slipping the dress over my body, I tied the belt around my waist and inspected myself. It hugged my curves nicely and draped in all the right places. The overall effect wasn't too bad; in fact, it was quite the transformation. I ran a brush through my hair, put on some makeup, and finished off the look with some strappy sandals.

"You clean up all right, Hadley," I said to my reflection.

"You sure do," Stella agreed as she came into my room. "You definitely don't look old enough to be my mother."

"Thanks, baby. I guess I look presentable enough." I shrugged. "You look stunning as always."

Stella did a quick twirl, and her electric blue dress flounced out around her petite body. The color and style of the garment perfectly accentuated her ivory skin and strawberry hair. She was beautiful, and the smile on her face lit up the room.

"I brought jewelry for you to wear. I made this yesterday. You can be my walking advertisement," Stella said as she held out a jade green necklace. I lifted my hair and she clasped it around my neck.

"It's beautiful. It's perfect for this dress," I said with a smile.

"Where are we going?" Stella asked as we grabbed our purses and headed out the door.

"There's a really nice restaurant called Almandine's a couple of blocks away. I've never actually eaten there, but everyone always talked about it. It's been around for years."

"Perfect."

Stella and I walked arm in arm, our heels clicking in unison down the sidewalk. For a brief moment in time, we weren't the grieving family members of a recently deceased loved one. We were simply two women on their way to celebrate a wonderful milestone. It felt nice and normal, and I let myself bask in the feeling while it lasted.

I was beyond proud of my daughter, and it felt great to have the opportunity to celebrate her accomplishments. Things had been hard for us the past several months, and we needed to enjoy life for a minute, to cast off the heaviness and let a little light shine into our world. Dinner at a great restaurant was just the ticket.

We walked through the front door of Almandine's, and the hostess seated us right away. Stella and I sat on opposite sides of the round table, which was covered with a luxurious white linen tablecloth. A flickering candle burned in the center, and perfectly folded black cloth napkins lay next to the shiny silverware. A sprig of rosemary in a small vase sat next to the candle. The overall effect was simple, yet classy.

"This place is really nice, Mom." Stella nodded with approval as she looked around the restaurant.

"I've always wanted to eat here." I smiled. "Now you've given me the perfect opportunity."

Our server handed us each a leather-bound menu, filled our crystal glasses with water, and told us the dinner specials. When she left, we both sat quietly, perusing the options. I had just settled on the chicken parmesan when my nostrils flared as they picked up the intoxicating and all-too-familiar scent of cedar and citrus. There was no mistaking that smell. My stomach flipped, and I didn't even need to look up to know who was standing next to our table.

"Hadley, what a surprise to see you here," Mack's voice, smooth as whiskey, slid into the room. "You look absolutely beautiful."

Taking a deep breath, I placed my menu on the table and reluctantly met his eyes. He was wearing perfectly fitted navy dress pants and an ivory button-up shirt. The blue of the pants accentuated the stunning color of his eyes. His hair was still a little wet and curled playfully around his ears. He was clean shaven, and he flashed me that perfectly dimpled smile that unraveled me every time.

I nearly melted, and if my daughter hadn't been at the table, I probably would have. His overall vibe was masculine perfection, yet soft around the edges. I reminded myself to keep my mouth shut so I wouldn't drool. By anyone's definition, Mack Kinley was gorgeous.

"My mom seems to have forgotten how to speak, so I'll introduce myself." Stella laughed. "I'm her daughter, Stella."

She reached out her hand to shake Mack's, giving me a quizzical look in the process.

"It's nice to meet you, Stella. There's no question that you're Hadley's daughter. You look just like her."

"I get that a lot," Stella chuckled.

Finally finding my voice, I piped in, "I'm surprised to see you, Mack."

"The feeling is mutual." He grinned. "But it's a good surprise."

"Do—uh—do you—uh—come here often?" I stammered.

"I do, actually. My sister is the manager, and I'm a sucker for the chicken parmesan."

"My mom loves that, too. If I had to guess, I'd say that's what she's planning to order tonight," Stella joked.

"I suppose I'm predictable like that." I shrugged uncomfortably.

"I'd say you're anything but." He met my gaze, and I couldn't seem to look away.

"Would you like to join us, Mack? I'd love to hear about how you and my mom know each other," Stella offered, flashing me a mischievous grin.

"I don't want to intrude," Mack answered politely.

"Yes, Mack and I barely know each other," I added quickly.

Mack's face fell, and hurt flashed in his eyes. I instantly regretted my words.

"That was rude of me. Of course, Mack, you should join us," I amended my comment.

"I really don't want to intrude," he repeated, his voice several degrees cooler than before.

"You wouldn't be intruding at all. In fact, since this dinner is for me, I insist." Stella gestured toward one of the empty chairs.

Mack sat down uncertainly, glancing my way to gauge my reaction. I forced myself to smile. After all, he was my contractor. I could sit down to a civilized, professional dinner with him, couldn't I?

About that time, our server returned. We informed her we would be adding one more to the table, and she said hello to Mack, who she clearly recognized. We placed our orders, and Mack and Stella made small talk while I did my best to maintain my composure. I couldn't believe Mack was sitting at our table, having dinner with us. All I could think about was our kiss and how amazing his lips had felt on mine. My stomach felt anything but settled, and I doubted I would be able to eat a bite.

"So, this dinner is for you, Stella? What are you celebrating?" Mack asked curiously.

"I'm a jewelry designer, and a huge retailer contracted to sell my creations today. It's something I've been working for, so Mom brought me out to celebrate," Stella gushed, obviously happy about her achievement.

"Congratulations." Mack smiled. "That's big news for sure."

"Stella is a bit of an artistic genius," I added, smiling her way, happy to have the conversation centered upon my daughter.

"Well, I got my talent from you," Stella added.

"You're an artist?" Mack turned his gaze toward me. "You never mentioned that."

"That's because I'm not."

"Don't listen to her. Mom's a gifted painter. If she even put forth the tiniest bit of effort, she'd have galleries standing in line wanting to show her work," Stella insisted.

"But you've never done anything with your paintings?" Mack inquired, obviously interested.

"I had a lot of big dreams when I was younger, but then I had kids. My priorities changed," I replied dismissively, sipping my water.

"Looks like your kids are off grabbing their own dreams. Maybe it's time to focus on yours again," Mack suggested with a raised eyebrow.

The electricity between us crackled and zinged. Stella looked back and forth between the two of us inquisitively. I knew it was impossible not to see the chemistry between Mack and me. I looked away from him quickly, trying to regain my bearings and remind myself that I had to retain the façade of professionalism.

"I agree with you, Mack. I think it's time for my mom to turn her focus onto herself and her own dreams and desires. She deserves that after all these years," Stella chimed in.

"Stella—" I interjected.

"My mom has given her whole self to her family, and it's time for her to think about what she wants for a change," Stella said with a decisive nod.

What had gotten into my daughter? It was like she knew I felt a connection to Mack and was encouraging it.

"So, you never did tell me how the two of you know each other, Mom. Did you grow up in Cottage Brook together?" Stella asked, glancing back and forth from Mack to me.

"Mack is the contractor for Grandma's house," I answered, sticking to the truth, although not all of it.

"The one you met a couple of weeks ago?" She raised an eyebrow in question.

"Yes." I nodded uncomfortably.

"The one you met with just that one time?" Stella looked at me skeptically, clearly seeing through my flimsy explanation.

"Yes," I answered weakly.

"Wow, you two seem really comfortable with each other for only meeting once," Stella replied with a mischievous grin.

"Well, your mom is very easy to talk to, Stella," Mack cut in, obviously trying to save my sinking ship.

"She really is," my daughter replied with a smile, her eyes darting between Mack and me.

"And sometimes people just connect, don't you agree, Hadley?" Mack tilted his head and focused his gaze on me again.

"Yes, sometimes they do." I took a deep breath and tried to redirect the conversation. "By the way, Mack has some great ideas for Grandma's house. You should tell Stella about them."

The corners of his mouth turned up into a slight smirk, almost as if he knew I was sending the uncomfortable conversation on a detour. He looked at me for a couple more seconds, then turned his attention to Stella. He shared with her his vision for my mother's house, and I let my brain tune out while they discussed the renovations.

About that time, the server brought our dinners, and it was nice to have something to do with my mouth besides stick my foot in it. The less Mack and I talked to each other, the better. I didn't know how he had the ability to reduce me to putty in his hands, but he did. It was an uncomfortable and dangerous position to be in, especially in front of my daughter.

Stella and Mack talked easily throughout the rest of dinner. She seemed comfortable, and I realized he had a way about him that simply put people at ease. It was clearly one of his gifts. His warmth and compassion drew people in and made them feel safe.

When our plates were empty and had been cleared away by our server, she returned with the bill. Mack grabbed it from her before it hit the table. "My treat, ladies."

"We can't let you do that," I insisted.

"It is my pleasure. Besides, I'm getting the better end of the deal—dinner with the two most beautiful women in town. Plus, you saved me from another lonely meal. I swear, the servers in this place feel sorry for me because I always eat alone." Mack laughed.

"You're so kind," Stella gushed. "Mom, isn't he the sweetest?"

"Yeah, he really is," I answered quietly.

"I'll go take care of this," Mack said as he stood. "Stella, it was a treat to meet you. Congratulations on your latest business venture. And Hadley, I'll be starting work on your mother's house tomorrow."

"Tomorrow? I thought you said it would be next week at the earliest."

"I was planning to call you tonight and let you know that my schedule changed, and I can start right away. Running into you here saved me a phone call, I guess." He shrugged.

"Great, tomorrow is perfect." I smiled, happy that the remodeling could finally begin. "The sooner the better."

"Feel free to stop by and check out my work whenever you'd like. I wouldn't mind at all."

Mack's eyes met mine and I felt my insides sizzle again. He held my gaze for a couple of seconds before turning to leave. When he was gone, I expelled the breath I had apparently been holding.

"Um, what was that?" Stella turned toward me, her eyes wide.

"What was what?" I asked, feigning innocence.

"You could feel the electricity crackling between the two of you. I was afraid I might get caught in the crossfire from being too close." Stella laughed.

"Electricity? I don't know what you're talking about, Stella." I rolled my eyes at her, although I knew exactly what she meant.

"The man is clearly into you. He couldn't stop looking at you."

"Stella, I think that's your youthful romanticism kicking in. I'm a middle-aged woman," I argued, my cheeks growing hot.

"Well, Mack sure wasn't looking at you like a middle-aged woman," she giggled.

"I'm a widow, honey. And a recent one at that," I leveled at her.

"I know that, Mom." Stella reached across the table and gripped my hand. "And I know you miss Dad. I do too. We're always going to miss him. But surely you remember what it feels like to have a man flirt with you."

"Mack wasn't flirting," I denied.

"He so was."

"Oh, Stella, I was married to your dad for such a long time. I was younger than you when I married him. And he's gone now. I don't know what I'm supposed to do with that." I sighed.

"You're supposed to go on. You're supposed to live your life. That's what Dad would want you to do," Stella advised. "I know you're still grieving. You're going to be for a long time. But eventually, you'll have to move past it."

"I just don't know. I loved your father so much."

The truth of the words hit me hard, because the reality was that I did love Charlie, and I had since the first day we met. Yes, we had gone through a rough patch, but now I would never get the chance to know if we could have worked things out. I didn't know how to accept that, or if I should even try.

Stella and I walked back to the hotel arm in arm. I had no idea what I was supposed to do with the rest of my life. Stella wanted me to live it, to dive in and think of myself. The idea of focusing on my wants and needs was so foreign to me that I honestly didn't even know where to begin. My daughter wanted me to put myself first, but I didn't know how. Stella didn't understand that I had so much unresolved baggage surrounding Charlie's death. I wanted, more than anything, the chance to explain things to my husband, to tell him the truth. I hated the fact that I couldn't. Getting past that might be something I could never do.

CHAPTER FOURTEEN

I AWOKE THE NEXT MORNING STILL TIRED FROM my restless night. I had slept little, most of the hours spent caught in a series of horrible dreams from which there was no escape. Each one involved Charlie and highlighted my guilt over his death. The worst was when I got to experience over and over again the moment my husband's car made impact with the oncoming bus that ended his life. It was a dream I'd had nearly every night since his death. It haunted me, and truth be told, I often wondered if it was some sort of cosmic punishment for my lies.

Groaning, I rolled out of bed and headed to the shower, doing my best to push the horrific images to the back of my mind so I could function. It was a routine to which I'd become accustomed. I could barely remember what it felt like to awaken rested and refreshed.

Dressing quickly, I poked my head inside Stella's room. She was on the phone again, and mouthed the words, "I'm sorry," when she saw me.

I smiled at her reassuringly, whispered, "It's okay," and blew her a kiss.

Grabbing my purse, I headed out the door. My phone buzzed in my pocket, and I looked at the screen. It was a number with a Cleveland area code, and I was pretty sure it was the same one I'd had all those missed calls from when I first arrived in Cottage Brook. I debated on whether or not to answer, but in the end, I let it go to voicemail. I figured if it was a legitimate call, whoever it was would leave a message. But they didn't.

"Definitely a telemarketer," I decided.

Tossing my phone into my purse, I made my daily stop at the coffee shop, sipping my triple espresso as I drove toward Aunt Viv's house. I hadn't seen her in several days, and I knew it was time to pay her a visit. I might not want to see my mother, but Aunt Viv was another story.

Pulling into her circular drive, I jumped out of the car and knocked on her front door. The maid answered mid-knock, and I wondered if the woman simply sat by the front door waiting for visitors. She was certainly prompt about answering.

She led me to the sunroom, where Viv sat sipping her morning tea and reading the newspaper.

"Ms. Hadley, ma'am," the maid announced.

"Thank you, Janet," Viv replied. "That will be all."

"Yes, ma'am," Janet replied. With a curt nod, the woman left the room as quickly as she'd entered it.

"Such efficiency." I laughed.

"Janet has been with me for many years. We don't require a lot of words," Viv replied with a smile. "Come, sit with me. I'd offer you some tea, but I see you are already drinking coffee. Dreadful stuff."

"It's the elixir of life," I joked, lifting my travel mug in the air as I sat in the chair beside her.

"So, what have you been up to, dear? Tell me all the details of how you're settling into Cottage Brook life." Viv placed the newspaper on the table, then folded her hands in her lap and gave me her full attention.

"Well, the landscapers you recommended have been making progress, and the yard is looking so much better," I began. "They'll come and do the finish work after the remodel, but at least the place doesn't look like a jungle anymore."

"They are a wonderful crew—hard workers, reasonably priced—good choice."

"The contractor had a scheduling change and he's starting today."

"Who did you hire? You mentioned that you'd found someone, but never told me who it was."

"Kinley Home Remodeling," I answered, trying to keep the flush from my cheeks as Mack's face popped into my head.

"Ah, Mack Kinley. He's a looker, that one," Viv said, her eyes glinting mischievously.

"Aunt Viv!"

"What? I may be an old woman, but I'm not dead. I know when a man is nice to look at. Goodness, Hadley, it's almost as if you think I don't have eyes," Viv replied, stiffening her neck a little, clearly offended.

"I mean—I—I didn't mean to imply that you were old—or that you wouldn't know—I mean—I was just surprised you knew him," I stammered.

"I know everyone. And Mack Kinley is a good man. He's done some work around here for me. I would have recommended him myself if you'd asked my opinion," Viv explained. "Since you didn't, I'm curious to know how you found him?"

"Oddly enough, he lives next door to Mom's

house. I saw his truck in the driveway, called the number, and there he was." I shrugged.

"Very serendipitous," Viv smiled mysteriously. "Wouldn't you say?"

"I'm guessing you already knew he lived next door to Mom, didn't you?"

"Of course I knew, silly girl. There's little that goes on in this town that I don't know about," Viv replied with a dramatic wave of her hand. "So how did you and Mr. Kinley get along?"

"Get along? What do you mean? He's my contractor. What does it matter if we get along or not?"

"Oh, it doesn't matter at all. But I'm guessing you got along swimmingly. And I'm never wrong."

"He's my *contractor*," I repeated, emphasizing the word. "That's all. I wish everyone would stop thinking there's something more between us," I shot at her, my cheeks burning.

"Who else thinks that?"

"Stella. Last night at dinner she said he was flirting with me. And it's just not true," I blurted.

"Dinner? You had dinner with Mack Kinley?" Viv raised one eyebrow quizzically.

"No—I mean—yes—er—it wasn't planned. Stella and I were at dinner, and he showed up. He joined us and, well, it was nothing. It wasn't a big deal at all," I explained, knowing I was talking too much, yet not quite able to stop.

"No, it certainly doesn't seem like a big deal to me." She chuckled.

"It wasn't," I said petulantly.

"As Shakespeare said, 'the lady doth protest too much, methinks.'" Viv quoted.

"Don't go throwing Shakespeare at me, Aunt Viv," I warned, wagging my finger at her. "Mack Kinley is my contractor."

"So you've said." Viv smirked.

Unable to help myself, I continued, "Granted, he is very nice. In fact, he's one of the kindest people I've ever met. He's so easy to talk to. He just has this amazing calming energy about him. And he's undeniably handsome. Like you said—a real looker. And... well... if I were looking for someone, he would definitely be the kind of man I'd be looking for. But... well... I'm not looking... and... he's just my contractor."

"Yes, dear," she agreed.

"Everyone seems to be forgetting that I lost my husband."

"No one has forgotten Charlie, darling, least of all, you." Viv leaned forward to pat my hand. "But

Charlie is gone, and you are here. Wouldn't he want you to be happy?"

"I don't know what Charlie would want. He's not here to tell me," I answered, my lip quivering and my eyes filling with tears.

"If he loved you, he would want you to be happy," she stated matter-of-factly. "Did Charlie love you, Hadley?"

"Yes. He did. He really did." I wiped my eyes with the corner of my sweater. "And I don't think I deserved it."

"Darling, you've never believed yourself worthy of love, which isn't your fault. It's the way you were raised. But you are a kind, loving, selfless person. You always put others first. If anyone deserves to be loved, and loved well, it is you." Viv paused, seemingly pondering her next words. "I didn't know your husband, but I am willing to bet that he would agree with me. To know you is to love you, so I'm certain that Charlie loved you."

"But what if I did something? Something terrible. Something unforgivable."

I so badly wanted to unburden myself. Carrying around the guilt was nearly tearing me apart. Could I confide in Aunt Viv? What would happen if I spoke the words out loud?

"I can't imagine you doing anything terrible, Hadley."

"But what if I did?"

My heart pounded and I wiped my sweaty palms on my jeans.

"Then maybe you need to tell someone about it. Carrying around a secret only makes it bigger."

I contemplated her words. I loved Aunt Viv, and I trusted her. She had always been there for me. But I couldn't help but be worried about her reaction. I didn't want her to think I was an awful person, even if I was.

"Darling, you can tell me anything. My feelings for you won't change," Viv encouraged, as if she could read my mind.

Taking a deep breath, I blurted, "What if I hurt Charlie? Like, really hurt him?"

Viv looked at me for a few seconds, watching intently as if she were measuring her words before she spoke, calculating how they might be received. After a pause, she answered, "Then I would say that I know exactly how you feel."

"What? How could you possibly know how I feel?"

"Because I've been there. I wasn't always the perfect wife," she hinted. "I did things I'm not proud of. I hurt my husband. In fact, I hurt him deeply. I was unfaithful."

"You mean? You—"

"That's exactly what I mean. And your uncle and I worked through it. People often do." Viv shrugged.

"You had an affair?" I shook my head, not quite able to believe she was telling the truth.

"I did. I'm not proud of it, but now that you know, do you feel any differently about me? Does it suddenly make me a horrible person?"

"No. It doesn't change anything. Nothing at all," I said quietly.

"So, you see, Hadley, I know that you can hurt people, often deeply, and they can still love and forgive you."

"The thing is, I didn't actually have an affair," I began.

"I didn't assume you had, dear," Aunt Viv smiled.

"But I did have feelings for another man—confusing, conflicting, crazy feelings. But I didn't act on them," I explained.

"So why do you feel so guilty? Marriage is hard work. Relationships go through ups and downs. Our feelings ebb and flow. Things become complicated.

But having feelings doesn't make you guilty. It makes you human. It's what you do with those feelings that matters."

"But you don't understand." I stood from the chair and began to pace.

"Understand what?"

"It's my fault that Charlie is dead."

"Were you driving the car?" Viv inquired.

"No. I wasn't."

"Were you driving the bus?"

"No."

"Were you even in the car?"

"No, I was at home."

"Then I fail to see how any of this is your fault."

Viv's calmness grated on my nerves.

"I told Charlie I was having an affair," I admitted.

"What?"

"I said the words to him, even though they weren't true. I said it to shock him. I wanted to hurt him to make myself feel better about the fact that I couldn't stop thinking about another man," I cried.

"Oh, Hadley." The compassion in Viv's voice nearly broke me.

"I told Charlie I was with another man," I said, cringing as I spoke the truth.

"Words can be forgiven. Didn't you explain yourself?"

"You don't understand!"

By that time, I was frantic, pacing the floor, crying, and beating myself up all over again.

"Hadley, if it wasn't true, then why do you feel so guilty?"

"Because those were the last words I ever said to Charlie," I sobbed, collapsing back into the chair. "I told him I was unfaithful. Then he ran out of the house. He drove his car into a bus. Viv, he died believing that I had cheated."

My body was racked with sobs by that point, and I didn't even have the strength to try to stop them. Viv scooted her chair closer to mine and gripped both my hands in hers. She didn't say anything. She just sat there and let me cry until the tears ran out.

"Now do you understand?" I asked, looking at her helplessly.

"I think I do. You blame yourself for a moment of weakness that I'm sure Charlie would have forgiven if he had lived long enough to hear the truth."

"But the fact is that I did have feelings for another man," I countered. "Isn't that just as bad?"

"Oh, darling, you hold yourself to an impossibly high standard. Do you think you're the first woman to have conflicting feelings about a man who isn't her husband? I hate to disappoint you, but it happens all the time," Viv answered. "That makes you guilty of nothing but being a confused human."

"How do you figure?"

"Let's say that Charlie hadn't died that day. Let's pretend instead that he got angry, took off, and eventually cooled down and came home, at which point the two of you had a good long conversation about what was really going on in your marriage," Viv began.

"Okay...."

"Once the two of you talked things through, you would have come to one of two conclusions—that you loved each other and wanted to work things out, or that your marriage had run its course and you were both going to move on. You had done nothing up to that point that was unforgivable."

"Do you really believe that?"

Viv had such a way of laying things out in the most rational, reasonable way possible. I had never considered things from that angle. I had been too wrapped up in guilt to see anything else.

"I really do believe that, Hadley. You see, unlike me, you never acted on your feelings. That, my dear, is something you can never take back. It's something that is very hard to forgive, and it takes a lot of years and a lot of therapy to get past."

"Thank you for trusting me with your secret." I squeezed her hand tightly. "And for making me see things a bit differently."

"Try not to be so hard on yourself. You've always been your own worst critic."

"It's just that there are so many things about myself to criticize." I laughed derisively.

"Oh, Hadley, I wish, for just one second, you could look at yourself and see what I see, what your daughters see, what I know your husband saw. You would be amazed at the view."

"I love you, Aunt Viv."

"And I love you, my dear."

"How's Mom doing?" I changed the subject. "I feel like I should go up to see her, but I'm not sure I have it in me."

"She's much the same. And I wouldn't recommend a visit today, not with your state of mind. Seeing Charlotte won't improve that."

"You're probably right. I'm reminding myself not to feel guilty about it," I answered.

"Darling, if you didn't feel guilt, would you have any feelings at all? I fear you've grown so accustomed to the emotion that you wouldn't recognize yourself without it."

"Maybe you're right." I shrugged, not sure what else to say.

"Sooner or later, Hadley, you have to let the guilt go. It serves no purpose. We all make mistakes, and we all do things we wish we could change. Bogging ourselves down with guilt and remorse simply robs us of the rest of our lives. If I could give you anything, it would be to absolve you of all that unnecessary guilt you feel."

"I'm working on it," I replied.

"Work harder." Viv smiled. "Forgive yourself."

"I'm going to head over to Mom's house and see if the crew has started yet." I gave Viv's hands one last squeeze and stood.

"That is a wonderful idea. I'll see you to the door."

Viv headed toward the foyer, and I followed, glancing up the stairs toward the part of the house where my mother was. No, I didn't have it in me to see her.

"Thanks for everything, Viv. It felt nice to finally unburden myself to someone," I said as I hugged her tightly.

"I am here for you. Always."

"I know you are. I appreciate that more than you can imagine."

Giving her a little wave, I headed toward my car.

"Oh, Hadley," Viv called.

"Yes?" I turned toward her.

"Say hello to Mack for me," she answered with a devilish grin.

"You are incorrigible." I laughed.

"I am, aren't I?" She smirked.

CHAPTER FIFTEEN

DRIVING TO MY MOTHER'S HOUSE, I REVISITED my conversation with Aunt Viv. Her wisdom centered me. She always gave such solid advice, and she had a way of making me take a closer look at everything and seeing it for what it was. I had been shocked to learn that her marriage had withstood the ramifications of an affair. I would have never guessed that Viv had been unfaithful to her husband. I supposed it was true that no one really knew what went on behind the scenes in a relationship.

I thought of Charlie and all the years I had loved him. He had been the center of my world for such a long time, and I was floundering without him by my side. I wondered what would have happened if Charlie hadn't died that day. Would he have been able to get past my feelings for Mack? Would I? Would Charlie have forgiven me for my secret?

Then a new thought entered my mind—Charlie had had a secret of his own. I'd been beating myself up about my lie, but he had also been dishonest with me. He'd destroyed our finances with a gambling problem I hadn't even known existed until after his death. Maybe the rift between us hadn't been one-sided at all. Charlie had grown distant because he was keeping secrets from me, and because of that distance, I sought out a connection with someone else.

It wasn't that I was trying to shift the blame to Charlie in order to make myself feel better. I knew I was equally at fault for our problems. But perhaps it was time to admit that the blame wasn't all mine. The problems Charlie and I had were because of both of us. Charlie was a good husband, but in all honesty, he was no more perfect than I was.

If he had lived, we might have worked everything out. Then again, maybe we wouldn't have been able to. The truth was, I would never know, and that was the part that was hard to accept. I wanted Charlie to give me absolution for my sins. I wanted to do the same for him. I wished more than anything that we'd had the chance to talk it out. But realizing the blame wasn't all mine lifted a huge weight off my shoulders. At least I had that.

Pulling into the driveway at my mother's house, I turned off the car. The landscapers were hard at work pruning an overgrown tree in the front yard, and a crew of workers was carrying trash, debris, and old furniture from inside the house and depositing it into the dumpster I'd rented. I couldn't believe how much better it looked already.

I didn't see Mack, but I guessed he was inside. Not wanting to disturb the workers, I walked around to the back door. Stepping inside the kitchen, I noticed Mack standing on a ladder scraping paint off the wall in the corner. Suddenly, my brain flashed back to me as a little girl, being thrown up against the wall of that same corner because I'd forgotten to put away my clothes before leaving for school. I'd sustained a serious concussion that day. The juxtaposition of Mack, happily scraping paint, and the image of my younger self smashing into that same wall was jarring.

Trying to push the horrible memory aside and center in on the present, I focused on Mack working, the muscles of his arms rippling as he scraped the paint. I was a little surprised to see him doing the actual work himself. For some reason, I'd assumed he just supervised. But seeing him on the ladder, lost in his work, he was certainly in his element.

There was music playing, and he was singing along, oblivious to everything, and clearly enjoying himself. His deep baritone voice sent shivers down my spine. His vocals were lovely, melodic, and smooth. I listened to him sing through the chorus of the song, realizing the sound gave me goose bumps. Starting to feel a bit like a voyeur, I thought perhaps I should announce my presence.

Not wanting to startle him, I cleared my throat. He turned his head, and his face broke into a huge smile when he saw me. He climbed down from the ladder, turned off the radio, and shoved his hands into his pockets.

"You're here." He locked his eyes onto mine. "I wondered if you'd stop by."

"I just wanted to check in. It looks like the wheels are in motion." I gestured around the room, trying not to look directly at him.

"We got an early start."

"Do you usually do the work yourself? I guess I thought your crew would do everything."

"Normally I just send out my men and supervise," he answered. "But this job is different."

"It is?"

"Sure." He shrugged. "It's next door to my house, so I want to be sure it's done right. After all, I have to look at it every day."

"Oh yeah, of course. I never thought of that."

Had a part of me been hoping he would say something else?

"But that's not the only reason, Hadley," he added with a grin.

"It's not?" My heart rate sped up considerably.

"I love getting in there and getting my hands dirty. It's why I went into the business to begin with."

"Right, yeah."

Of course his reasons have nothing to do with you, Hadley. Don't flatter yourself.

"And getting the chance to see you every day is just an added bonus."

His eyes focused in on me with laser precision. I nervously chewed the skin around my nails, trying to look away but finding I couldn't.

"Mack—"

"Yeah, yeah, I know, we're going to keep it professional and all that jazz," he laughed.

"Yes. Professional." I swallowed hard, telling my heart to slow down.

"But I've got to admit that I can't stop thinking about that kiss."

"Mack—"

"And, you know, that's great if you want to play things that way. I'll abide by your rules. But just so you know, my feelings for you are anything but professional."

"Feelings—for me—" I stammered.

"Surely you've figured out by now how I feel about you, Hadley. I've been pretty transparent."

"Mack—"

"I know you're not ready for anything, and I get it. I know your life is crazy and chaotic, and you're still grieving the loss of your husband. I understand all that," Mack said.

"You do?"

"Of course I do. Remember, I lost my wife several years ago."

"That's right. She had cancer."

"It was the darkest time of my life, and I remember thinking I'd never get over it."

"But you did."

"Yeah, eventually."

He walked across the room and stood in front of me, close enough to touch me, but he didn't.

"I would never push you. If you want to be

friends, then I'll be the best friend you've ever had. If you want more, all you have to do is say the word."

"You would do that? You would wait?"

"For you? Oh yeah." He smiled.

"I don't know what to say."

"Listen, Hadley, that day in the coffee shop, something just clicked for me. I knew you were exactly what I'd been waiting for. When you took off without even telling me your name, I didn't know if I'd ever see you again. So, I left it all up to fate. I told myself that if we were meant to be together, somehow it would all work out."

"You did?"

"Yes. I've thought of you every single day for more than a year. When I opened your mother's door and saw you standing there, it was like a miracle."

"It is pretty crazy the way things worked out," I admitted.

"Crazy? I think it's fate. Think about it—we met at a coffee shop far away from here, didn't know each other's names, and had this insane connection. I couldn't stop thinking of you and wishing I knew where to find you. Then, one day, over a year later, I went to a job next door to my own house and there you were. If that's not destiny, I don't know what is," Mack explained.

"You're a bit of a romantic, aren't you?" I smiled.

"Guilty as charged." He shrugged. "Look, maybe the timing isn't right, and that's okay. But I want you in my life in whatever way you're willing to be there."

"And what if I say I don't want to be in your life at all?" I challenged, my heart pounding in my chest.

"Then I would have to call you a liar. I know you feel a connection between us," he stated matter-of-factly.

"Fine, you're right, Mack. I do," I admitted. "But I don't know what to do with that."

"I know you don't. And that's okay. Eventually you will."

I hesitated. "So, we can be friends?"

"I'll be whatever you want me to be, Hadley."

The intense look in his eyes caught me off guard. A warmth radiated in my middle, and I suddenly felt lightheaded. I reached out and grabbed Mack's hand, giving it a firm shake.

"Friends," I said with a grin, knowing deep inside that it was way more than that.

"Friends," he repeated. "For now."

"Great," I replied, biting my lip nervously.

"And as your friend, I think you need a night of

fun. How about dinner and a movie after I finish up here for the day?"

The hopeful look on his face melted my heart. I couldn't bring myself to tell him no.

"That actually sounds a lot like a date," I teased. "Not that I've had one in a really long time."

"You clearly don't remember dating. This would be nothing like a date. I promise." He grinned.

"Okay," I agreed. "As long as it's not a date."

"You have my word. I'll see you at seven o'clock." Mack winked.

CHAPTER SIXTEEN

AFTER LEAVING MY MOM'S HOUSE, I HEADED back toward the hotel, a smile on my face that I couldn't seem to wipe away. I was amazed at how much better I felt after talking to Aunt Viv that morning, and the conversation with Mack had helped to further buoy my spirits. We had come to an agreement, Mack and I, and we were in a really good place. I could use a friend, and even though I knew Mack wanted more, I was sure he wouldn't push me.

Driving through town, I came to a stop sign. Glancing to my left I saw a store I'd never noticed before. It was called The Artist's Gallery, and on a sudden whim, I pulled my car into a parking spot and went inside. The shopkeeper nodded at me and said hello, telling me to ask any questions I might have.

I wandered through the aisles, breathing in the scent of paint as a thousand emotions swirled around inside of me. I ran my fingertips over the palettes, gently touched the paintbrushes, and let my eyes absorb the rainbow of paint colors. It had been years since I'd picked up a brush, but in that moment, I felt the compulsion to paint. I hadn't experienced the desire in such a long time, but right then, it was something I had to do. I needed to create like I needed to breathe.

I knew that I should conserve my money, and paint supplies were a frivolity I couldn't afford, but the need was so intense I didn't even try to push it aside. I grabbed an easel, a variety of paints, brushes, a few canvases, a paint palette, drop cloth, and a rag for cleanup.

Almost reverently, I placed my supplies on the counter, my heart pounding inside my chest. Expelling a large breath when I heard the total, I handed the shopkeeper my credit card, then carried my precious loot to the car, telling myself not to think about the money.

My hands were shaking as I got behind the wheel and headed to the hotel. The image had come to me as I was standing in the art store, and I knew I needed to paint it. The picture in my brain was as real to me as my own heartbeat, and the need to create it was more intense than anything I'd felt in years. Several times I'd had ideas, but I'd always pushed them down, reminding myself that I didn't have time for such things. My daughters had always come first.

But now—I couldn't even explain how strong the impulse was. I knew the image would claw at me until I unleashed it onto the canvas. I hadn't painted for such a long time, and the idea of doing it again was terrifying. Yet I knew I had to.

The truth was, I knew I had talent. Some of the work I'd done decorated the walls of our house in Cleveland, and visitors always complimented it. But it was so long ago that a part of me wondered if I still had the gift. Self-doubt crept in, telling me what I was about to do was ridiculous, but I didn't even care. I was going to paint again, and nothing else mattered.

Pulling into the parking lot of the hotel, I grabbed the supplies and headed upstairs to my room. Stella's bedroom door was closed, and I heard her faint voice on the other side, presumably talking to a client. Dropping my purse onto the table, I carried everything else into my room, closing the door behind me and locking it tightly.

My palms were sweating, and my heart was pounding, but the excitement and current of energy I remembered so well coursed through my body. I adjusted the drop cloth on the floor. Setting up the easel, I propped up the canvas and selected my paints and brushes.

When everything was prepared, I stripped off my clothing and threw on old sweats and a ratty T-shirt. I tossed my hair into a messy bun and turned on the radio. I stood there, letting the music wash over me, imagining myself painting, reminding myself that I still knew how.

Walking toward the easel, I selected my brush, dipping it into the red paint. The picture in my mind was more vivid than anything I'd ever seen before. I had to let it out. Closing my eyes, I took a deep breath and counted to ten. Opening my eyes, I smiled as I touched my brush to the canvas.

SOMEWHERE IN THE BACK OF MY MIND, I HEARD knocking. I ignored it, trying to push it into the background, but it grew louder. Stella's voice on the other side of the door finally got my attention.

"Mom, hey, are you okay in there?"

Blinking my eyes, I resurfaced in the present, recognizing that I had been transported somewhere else for a very long time. I remembered the feeling of leaving my body, of becoming so consumed by my work that the rest of the world ceased to matter. It had been ages since I'd experienced it, but the second I'd begun painting, the muse had taken over.

A bit disoriented, I looked around the room, realizing it had grown dark. The sun was no longer shining outside, and the streetlights had come on somewhere along the way. There was paint splattered all over my clothes, and my hands were covered with a hodgepodge of colors from where I'd used my fingers to add texture to the picture.

"Mom, if you don't answer the door right now, I'm going to break it down," Stella yelled. "You're freaking me out."

Walking quickly toward the door, I called out, "Sorry baby, I didn't mean to worry you. I was—doing—a thing."

I swung open the door, a huge smile on my face. Shock and confusion replaced the smile when I saw

Mack standing next to Stella. Both of their faces reflected their apparent concern.

"Mack—what are you doing here?"

"You said we would go on that non-date thing tonight, remember?" He smiled slowly, taking in my appearance.

"Yeah, I do remember. I guess the day just sort of got away from me," I replied, glancing down at the paint on my hands.

"Are you *painting*, Mom?"

"Well, I was, uh—" I began.

"I mean, I didn't want to bother you, but after hours of you being locked behind the door, I was getting worried."

"I'm sorry, honey. I didn't mean to worry you."

"And then Mack showed up for something he very clearly said was not a date... which I still don't really believe... and, well..." Stella trailed off, confusion all over her face.

"It's definitely not a date, Stella," Mack interjected. "Right, Hadley?"

"Right. And I swear I didn't forget. I just got... sidetracked."

"Sidetracked with what? Have you been painting your hotel room, Mom? Is that even allowed?" Stella craned her neck to look around me and into the room.

"I wasn't painting the hotel room—but I was—painting," I admitted shyly.

"Painting? Like creating artwork? Mom, that's fantastic!" Stella squealed, reaching out to hug me.

"I have to admit that it felt pretty fantastic." I beamed.

"Can I see it?" Stella asked excitedly.

"Yes, I'd love to see it too, Hadley. That is, if you don't mind," Mack added.

"See it? I don't know...."

I balked at the idea of sharing something as personal as my art with Mack, although I had no idea why, since he already knew so much about me. Somehow, Mack looking at my art was the equivalent of him seeing me naked.

"I know artists don't like to show things before they're done, but I'd love to see what you have so far," Mack said, gently laying his hand on my arm.

"I'd love to see it too, Mom," Stella added.

"I can't believe I'm saying this, but yes, you can see it. Both of you. I'm really proud of it. And it's actually finished." I shrugged. "I don't know what time it is, but I've been at it for hours."

"It's almost seven thirty," Mack answered. "And you have a little paint on your nose."

He reached out his finger and lightly touched the side of my nose. Self-consciously, I reached up and picked at the caked-on paint.

"Oops." I rolled my eyes.

"Don't worry about it. You look adorable, all covered in paint," Mack added, his blue eyes glinting mischievously.

"She does, doesn't she? It suits her." Stella grinned. "Now, let's get to the good stuff. I've been waiting years to see you paint again, so show it to me."

Turning on my heel, I walked across the bedroom toward the easel, with Stella and Mack in my wake. I looked at the painting, trying to view it with an impartial eye. I tried hard, but there was no way for me to be objective. All I could see was a chunk of my soul on the canvas.

Stella gasped when she saw it, and Mack blew out a sustained breath. Both of them looked at it for several seconds, neither saying a word. I watched as they took in the colors, shading, textures, and nuances of the painting. I wondered if they, too, could see my soul on the canvas.

Finally, after a few moments of silence, Stella

reacted. She turned toward me, tears in her eyes, and wrapped her arms around me, hugging me tightly.

"This is stunning, Mom. I don't even have words to describe how I feel when I look at it. It's like—all the facets of happiness and sadness wrapped up in one image. You've perfectly captured both of those feelings."

"I'm overwhelmed by your talent, Hadley. I had no idea you could do this," Mack said quietly, still looking at the painting. "You truly have a gift."

"What's it called?" Stella asked, wiping her eyes as the tears flowed freely.

"I named it *Hope Swallows Grief*," I replied, my voice shaking a little.

A feeling of complete satisfaction washed over me as I looked at what I'd created. The image was an anatomically correct heart. One half was painted as a barren desert, with the distinct feeling of death and decay. The other half bloomed with colorful flowers, creeping past the middle, toward the bleak half, bits of color and small flowers popping up here and there, trying to grow in the desert.

It was the way I saw my own heart, and I knew I'd depicted it perfectly.

CHAPTER SEVENTEEN

"I KNOW YOU'VE HAD A BUSY, EMOTIONAL DAY, but are you still up for dinner and a movie?" Mack asked when we finally headed out into the living room.

"Dinner and a movie?" Stella raised one eyebrow. "That definitely sounds like date material."

"Nope, not a date." Mack grinned widely. "My plan is for your mother and me to have zero fun, and you have to have fun on a date... so... that means this is not a date, like I said."

"You can't fool me, either one of you." Stella put her hands on her hips and stared me down.

"We're not trying to fool anyone," I insisted, trying not to smile.

"Keep on denying your feelings, but I can see

through you both," Stella chuckled. "I'm off to take a long hot bath after a stressful day at work. But don't worry—I won't wait up."

My face turned red. "Mack and I are not denying any feelings, Stella. We've settled all that—we've decided to be friends."

"Uh-huh. Whatever you say, Mom. I think I'll give Celeste a call tonight. I'll tell her you're painting again, and definitely not dating. Oh, and that you have a handsome new *friend*." With a wink, Stella gave us a sassy little wave and headed to her room.

"Sorry about my daughter." I shook my head. "I don't know what's gotten into her lately."

"She loves you. She wants you to be happy. Seems pretty simple to me," Mack answered.

"Anyway, I'm really sorry you showed up here and I'm all covered in paint. I swear I didn't forget that we had plans. I just... lost track of time."

"It's no wonder. You had very important work you were doing today. Seriously, Hadley, I'm amazed at your talent. I can't believe you can paint like that."

"It's nothing." I waved my hand, embarrassment creeping in.

"It's definitely *not* nothing. You could sell that at a gallery, no problem," Mack said. "I think you should seriously consider it."

"I can't approach a gallery with only one painting." I laughed.

"Don't you have others?"

"Well, yes, I do. I have several that I painted when I was younger," I answered, mentally counting the paintings in my house in Cleveland.

"And you can paint more too. You're clearly able to." He gestured toward my room.

"Maybe." I shrugged. "I don't know. What I really need to do is find an actual job, to make real money."

"People would pay real money for what I just saw in there." He gestured toward my room. "You need to keep doing it, and then you need to sell them."

"I don't know, Mack. I need a reliable income, and art isn't reliable."

"I think you're underestimating yourself again. But I'll keep working on you." He smiled. "By the way, we can totally skip the movie if you'd rather just do dinner and a walk or something. It's a really nice night."

"That sounds great, actually. Give me ten minutes to change out of these clothes," I said as I went to my room.

I threw on jeans and a sweater, washed the paint off my face, touched up my makeup, and took my hair out of the bun, running a brush through it. The strawberry waves cascaded down my back. I was glad it didn't take much effort for it to look good, as I wasn't one to mess with my hair. Glancing at my watch, I saw that I had transformed myself in only seven minutes, three minutes less than I promised Mack.

"All ready." I smiled as I rejoined him in the living room. "And in only seven minutes."

"No way." He shook his head in surprise. "I've never known a woman who could get ready in under ten minutes. Of course, you could roll out of bed and do absolutely nothing and still knock my socks off, so there's that."

"You're very kind," I answered, my face flushing at his compliment.

"I'm just an honest man."

"Are you ready to go?"

"Absolutely."

I grabbed my purse, called goodbye to Stella, and Mack and I left the hotel. We walked to the parking lot, and I looked around for his work truck, but didn't see it.

"Where's your truck?" I asked.

"At home. I drove my car tonight, since I'm not working. I hope you don't mind."

He gestured toward the shiny silver Camaro in the nearest parking space. It looked brand-new, and the sleek lines and sparkling paint job made me catch my breath. It was beautiful, and I had always been a sucker for sports cars, even though I'd never owned one.

"This is your car?"

"Yep, that's my baby," he answered proudly.

"It's amazing. I love it."

"Well, your chariot awaits, milady." He gave an exaggerated bow and opened the passenger door, gesturing me inside.

Laughing, I shook my head as he shut the door.

Of course, he would have a sports car. Why wouldn't he? Mack Kinley was practically perfect in every way.

Backing out of the parking lot, Mack pulled onto Main Street. "I thought we would drive over to Landsbury for dinner if that's okay. There's a great little restaurant there, and then we can take a walk on the nature trail. As long as that's okay with you."

"That sounds great. I haven't been to Landsbury in years," I replied, sinking into the plush leather seat.

Landsbury was the next town over, and about twenty miles away. It would be nice to get out of Cottage Brook for a while and do some exploring. Mack and I rode in companionable silence, listening to the radio. Neither of us felt the need to fill the moments with unnecessary words. We were comfortable in each other's presence, the kind of easy comradery that was unusual and hard to find. I hadn't felt that relaxed in a very long time.

"I guess I should have asked if you like pizza," he said when we pulled up in front of the restaurant. "I mean, I'm pretty sure everyone likes pizza, and if you don't, I probably need to question our friendship."

"Pizza happens to be my favorite food." I laughed. "No need to question our friendship quite yet."

I followed Mack inside the building, and we seated ourselves in a circular booth in the back corner, away from the hustle and bustle of the rest of the room. A server approached us right away. She was a stunning, twentysomething blonde woman who flashed Mack a wide grin that showed off her perfect teeth.

"Hey, Mack, good to see you," she practically purred as she placed our menus in front of us.

"Hey, April. This is Hadley," he answered good-naturedly, gesturing toward me.

"Hi," she said, a touch of irritation in her voice.

"It's nice to meet you, April." I smiled kindly.

"What can I get you to drink?" She directed the question to both of us, but her eyes were focused in on Mack.

"I'll take a beer," Mack answered, looking at me. "Hadley?"

"Red wine for me," I added.

"Sure thing. I'll be back to take your order in a bit."

April was clearly aggravated that she couldn't catch Mack's attention. She flashed me an angry look, turned on her heel, and walked away. I got the distinct impression that she had a thing for Mack, and she didn't like the fact that he was sitting at the table with me.

"An old flame of yours?" I raised an eyebrow.

"Not even. I have turned her down—as politely as possible, I might add—several times." He laughed.

"She's very pretty. And young. Why did you turn her down?"

"April's not my type."

"Oh really? And what's your type?"

Mack scooted closer to me in the booth. He

leaned in and moved my hair away from my ear, brushing my cheek with his fingertips in the process. My heart rate sped up considerably, and the air thickened around us.

"I like fortysomething strawberry blonde painters that I meet in random coffee shops. I have a very specific type," he said quietly.

"You're pretty smooth, you know that?" My body tingled as the scent of his cologne wafted into my nostrils.

"I'm just honest, Hadley." He leaned away, giving me space once again.

The way he said my name made me dizzy. My head was spinning, and I kept telling myself I only wanted to be his friend, although at that moment, I had no idea why. I loved being with him, and even in moments when my physical response to him left me reeling, it was so good. Being with Mack felt right. Kissing him had felt better than anything I could have imagined. As much as I tried to fight it, I had to admit there was nowhere else I'd rather be than sitting right there next to him.

After a few moments, April returned with our drinks. She took our orders and headed back toward the kitchen. As organically as always, Mack and I slipped back into casual, comfortable conversation. Talking with him was as easy as breathing.

I sipped my wine, and Mack nursed his beer. For some reason, I had been worried that dinner would be uncomfortable, too much like a date, but there had been no need for my concern. We were every bit as much at ease with each other as we'd been the first time we met. Every time I was with him, it only got better.

It wasn't long before our pizza arrived, and we munched on it while we talked about everything under the sun. We had just finished eating when my phone buzzed. I intended to see who it was and let it go straight to voicemail, but when Aunt Viv's name flashed across the screen, something told me to answer it.

"I'm sorry, I have to grab this," I said as I answered.

"Go ahead." Mack nodded.

As soon as I heard Aunt Viv's voice, I knew something was wrong. I assured her that I would be there as soon as I could and hung up the phone.

Turning to Mack, my voice trembled. "I—I have to go. I'm—sorry—but it's my mom. They don't think she'll make it through the night."

CHAPTER EIGHTEEN

Mack paid the bill quickly, and we rushed outside and jumped into the car. Pulling out of the parking lot, he sped back toward Cottage Brook as fast as the speed limit would allow.

"I—I'm so sorry—" I stammered. "I didn't mean to ruin the night."

A thousand warring thoughts fought it out inside my brain. I wasn't sure what to say. I didn't even know how I felt.

"Hadley, please don't apologize. Not to me. I can't imagine what you're feeling right now." Mack reached over and took my trembling hand into his.

The warmth of his skin wrapped itself around the coldness of mine. Our fingers intertwined felt perfectly right. I wanted to absorb everything good he had inside him. I wanted him to chase away the darkness for me, because at that moment, it felt like it might swallow me whole.

"You know I'm right here, Hadley. You can talk to me if you need to. Sometimes it helps to let it out," he offered.

"I don't even know what I'm feeling, Mack."

"I know. You don't have to," he assured me.

"I'm supposed to be overcome with sadness or something, right? But I'm just not. All I feel is numb," I admitted, a bit ashamed of my lack of emotion. "Does that make me a terrible person?"

"There's no right or wrong way you're supposed to deal with this. You feel what you feel. Don't question it or try to justify it."

"Old habits die hard," I said quietly.

"Look, the relationship you have with your mom is complicated, Hadley. There's nothing normal about it, so why would you expect to feel something normal? What is normal, anyway?"

"It's just that—when I found out she was sick—I had this fleeting moment of—I don't know—thinking that maybe we could iron things out before she died," I tried to explain.

"That's a reasonable thing to wish, I think," he answered, squeezing my hand tightly.

"But the thing is—that hasn't happened. And I haven't tried very hard to make it happen."

"And that's okay. It doesn't have to happen. Some things are just too broken to fix," he advised.

"Do you really believe that? Or are you just trying to make me feel better?"

"I believe it," he said.

"I wish—I guess I don't know what I wish." I shrugged helplessly.

Mack was silent for a couple of seconds, and I got the distinct feeling that he was weighing the words he was about to say. After a brief silence, he spoke.

"Hadley, from what you've told me, your mother abused you and treated you in a way that no parent should ever treat a child. The fact that you emerged from that and made yourself into the amazing woman sitting in my car is nothing short of a miracle in my book."

"And you really think it's okay if we never make amends?"

"Do you want to know what I think? For real?"

"Yeah, Mack, I really do."

"I think your mom's reaction or response at this point doesn't matter. She's going to die. The only thing that matters is you—what do you need to be able to come out on the other side of this in one piece?" he began.

"Go on," I encouraged, curious to hear what else he had to say.

"I think that forgiving your mom is important for you and for your future. It doesn't matter if she can hear you, or even if she accepts it. But I think if you can look at the woman who tried to destroy your life and forgive her before she dies, well, then you'll be free."

"Forgive her? I don't know. That's a big one, Mack." I shook my head. "I've told you a lot about my life with her, but there's so much more."

"This will be the biggest, hardest, most impossible thing you'll ever do. But if you can manage it, she'll no longer have a hold on you."

I nodded, pondering his words as we raced along the road. His compassion drew me in, wrapping me up like a warm hug. There was so much wisdom and kindness in him. I wanted to bottle it up and drink it down in an effort to absorb it into myself. I wanted to be good like him.

We made it to Aunt Viv's house in record time, and Mack pulled the Camaro into her driveway, jumped out, and helped me from the car.

"Do you want me to wait outside? I don't want to intrude," he offered as he walked me to the door.

"No, I don't want you to wait outside." I swallowed hard.

"Tell me what you want me to do," he said. "I'm here for you, however you need me."

"I—uh—I know it's asking a lot, but—uh—would you come with me? I don't know if I can face her alone," I answered, my lip quivering.

"Of course I'll come with you." He took my hand in his once again and squeezed it tightly. "I won't leave your side until you tell me to."

Janet answered the door on the first knock, ushering us quietly into the foyer where Aunt Viv was waiting. Her eyes widened when she saw Mack, but a contented smile turned up the corners of her mouth immediately.

"Hello, Mack," she greeted. "I'm so glad to see you here with Hadley."

"Hello, Vivian," he replied. "How are you holding up?"

"It's a hard night, that's for certain. Although we've all known it was coming for quite some time," she replied.

"That doesn't make it any easier," Mack replied compassionately.

"Hadley, I've called Stella, and she'll be here soon. I've sent a car for her. You should probably go on up. The doctor says it won't be long."

Mack gripped my hand a little tighter, and together we walked up the stairs toward my mother's room. My stomach was twisted in a thousand knots, and my knees were shaking. Mack seemed to sense my apprehension, and he let go of my hand and instead wrapped his arm around my shoulders, pulling my body close to his, basically holding me upright.

"I'm right here. I'm not going anywhere," he whispered as we walked through the door together.

The nurse wasn't in the room, and neither was the doctor. My mother was alone, lying in bed, her paper-thin eyelids closed. Her skeletal frame was so small. She looked even more diminished than the last time I saw her. She wasn't moving at all, and for a fleeting moment, I wondered if she was already dead.

Mack and I moved closer until we were standing at her side. The sight of her, so close to death, was nearly more than I could take. My quaking knees buckled beneath me. Mack tightened his grip, catching me, and lowered my body until I was sitting on the edge of the bed. Standing beside me, he took my hand in his and held it tightly.

"I don't know what to say to her," I whispered, tears spilling from my eyes. "I don't even know where to start."

"Just tell her what's in your heart," he encouraged. "Even if the words don't sound right."

Taking a deep breath, I tried to corral my thoughts. A thousand images of the two of us swirled around in my mind, each one of them a horrific reminder of our toxic relationship. I closed my eyes and searched for something—anything—good. All I needed was one non-painful memory to focus on. Yet I couldn't think of a single thing.

"Mom, I know things between us are hard," I began, hoping I would be able to find the right words.

As soon as she heard my voice, my mother's eyelids fluttered open, and she looked at me. She focused her glassy gaze on me for a minute, and I wasn't sure if she knew where she was or who I was. All of a sudden, a sense of clarity came over her, and I knew she recognized me. There was no question that she was there, in that moment, with me.

"Hadley," she said weakly.

"Mom—yeah, it's me—Hadley. I just wanted to —" I began.

"No. Don't say anything," she commanded, her voice growing stronger.

"But I wanted—"

"I know you were going to apologize, just like you always did when you were a little girl. But don't you dare say another word," she demanded.

"Mom—"

"Listen to me. You did nothing wrong. Ever. It was me. The drinking. All me. I was wrong. I hurt you. I was wrong."

She worked hard to get the words out, her voice straining and her breath coming in short spurts from the effort.

"Mom—"

"My little girl."

She looked at me for several moments, and for the first time in my life, I saw love in my mother's eyes. It was the one thing I had yearned for since I was a child, and in the final seconds of her life, she was giving it to me. The tears began slowly at first, then cascaded like waterfalls down my cheeks. All of the emotions I hadn't been able to feel washed over me at once. The frozen numbness of my heart began to thaw.

"I'm so sorry. For everything," my mother whispered, her voice growing weak again.

"I—forgive—you—" I sobbed, knowing I had to say the words before it was too late.

A whisper of a smile brushed across her face, and she closed her eyes. I watched her chest fall. Then I waited for it to rise, for her to take another breath, but she didn't. She'd been waiting for me all along. Blinking back the tears, I took a shuddering breath of my own and lifted my eyes toward Mack.

"She's gone."

CHAPTER NINETEEN

A WEEK LATER, WE BURIED MY MOTHER IN THE same cemetery where her parents and grandparents were laid to rest. I stood there, my daughters on either side of me, and I wept. I'd thought the years of pain and torture I'd experienced at my mother's hands had numbed me to the point that I was no longer capable of feeling anything for her, but her death had proven me wrong.

I had cried for my mother and our broken relationship every day since she passed away. The tears were cathartic. The ability to feel something other than anger for her had begun to mend my broken heart. I knew that our deathbed reconciliation had been a fork in the road for me, and I understood, without a doubt, that I'd chosen the right path in forgiving her.

I had painted three more pictures in the past week, each one more emotional than the last. Something had come over me, and I was feeling things more deeply than I ever had in my life. The barren wasteland of my heart was blooming once again. Painting had been the therapy I needed. It was helping me come to terms with my life and showing me how I could heal the broken pieces and put myself back together again.

Mack had been a lifeline for me as well—checking in on me every day, bringing me food, and making sure I was taking care of myself. Celeste had taken a leave of absence from work and was staying with Stella and me at the hotel. Having both my girls under the same roof again made my heart full and happy.

I was different, and I felt it in every cell of my being. Something was stirring, changing inside of me. I was like a caterpillar, nearly ready to emerge from my chrysalis, metamorphosed into a lovely butterfly. The change within me had been a long time coming, but it was real.

The minister's words brought me back to the moment at hand. "Romans 8:38-39 says, 'for I am convinced that neither death nor life, neither angels nor demons, neither the present nor the future, nor any powers, neither height nor depth, nor anything else in all creation, will be able to separate us from the love of God that is in Christ Jesus our Lord.'"

I let his words sink in, and I felt them deep within my soul. There was love all around me—from my daughters, Aunt Viv, and as much as I had tried to fight it, from Mack. I had felt so insignificant, completely invisible, for such a long time, but I didn't feel that way anymore. I was there, taking up space, and not apologizing for it. I was becoming the person I was meant to be—the one I had buried so thoroughly for all of those wasted years. Most importantly, I was hemmed in on all sides by undeniable, unconditional love.

It had taken the deaths of both my husband and my mother to open my eyes, but I was finally wide awake. I had a lot of people in my corner who believed in me. Maybe it was time to finally believe in myself.

When the graveside service was over and all the guests had gone, I stood in the cemetery with Mack and my daughters. I watched the three of them together. There was an easy comfortableness about them. It was like they had always known each other, as if they recognized in Mack a kindred spirit. It was exactly the way I felt when I was around him.

Mack Kinley had been occupying a lot of real estate in my brain since the moment I laid eyes on him. I thought of him relentlessly, especially lately, while I painted. It had taken me some time, but I had come to a very obvious conclusion—I was hopelessly, head over heels, one hundred percent in love with him.

I wasn't ready to tell him, and I wasn't ready to act on it. I liked the way things were between us. I adored the easy friendship we'd established. I didn't want anything to change that, and admitting my feelings to him would surely change everything.

So I decided to keep it to myself. There would be plenty of time for Mack and me to dive into that current somewhere down the road.

As I watched my daughters standing next to my mother's newly dug grave, a vivid image popped into my head. It was perfectly clear, and I knew I had to paint it. But it didn't belong on a canvas. I knew exactly where it needed to be.

"Can I drive you back to the hotel, Hadley? You look tired," Mack said, placing his arm around my shoulders.

"I actually have somewhere else I need to go," I

replied, the image growing clearer in my mind. "Can you drop me off at my mother's house? But I have to grab a few things from the hotel first."

"Sure. We'll drop the girls off at the hotel and then I'll take you. It's on my way." He smiled.

"Do you want us to go with you, Mom?" Celeste asked, joining in on the tail end of our conversation.

"Yeah, we can help you do whatever you need to do," Stella chimed in.

"No, not this. I need to do this alone," I said, hugging them both. "But thank you. I am so grateful to have my girls here with me."

Mack drove us to the hotel. I went into my room and grabbed my painting supplies, kissed my daughters goodbye, and got back into Mack's car.

When we arrived at my mom's house, he turned toward me. "I get the feeling that whatever you're stewing on is important and personal, so I'm not even going to ask if you want me to come inside."

"Thank you, Mack, for understanding," I said, my voice catching in my throat as my emotions swelled. "Really. Thank you for everything. I don't know how I would have made it through these last months without you. You've been my rock. Even when I tried to push you away."

"I'd do anything for you, Hadley," he said

quietly, reaching out to grab my hand. "I hope you know that by now."

"I know you would." I swallowed hard.

For a split second, I felt the need to tell him everything, for him to know my true feelings. I wanted to convey to him the depth of my emotions, to make him understand how grateful I was to have him in my life. I wanted to tell him I loved him, that I wanted to be with him, to share my life with him. But something held me back, and I wasn't sure why. For some reason, it didn't feel like the right time.

"Thank you for the ride," I said instead, opening the passenger door and sliding out.

"If you need anything, I'll be right next door. Let me know when you're ready to go back to the hotel and I'll drive you." He smiled.

"I don't think it'll be anytime soon. What I have to do is going to take a while. I texted the girls and told them not to expect me back tonight."

"You're sure you're okay in there alone? Overnight? I know being inside the house is difficult for you," Mack said gently.

"It is. But I need to do this. Hopefully, after tonight, everything will be different," I answered with a smile.

Giving him a little wave, I closed the car door

and went inside the house. Flipping on the light, I watched it illuminate the front hallway, chasing away the shadows. I walked from room to room, turning on all the lights as I went. I hadn't been there in over a week, and I was amazed at the progress Mack and his crew had made. It looked like they would be done before long.

When I reached the staircase, I slowly climbed each step, listening to the creak of the boards beneath my feet. My mind replayed a hundred memories of me walking up those stairs over the years. Most of the time it had been in an effort to escape my mother's wrath.

As each memory resurfaced, I leaned in, really feeling the emotion attached to it. As I remembered each moment, I forgave my mother once again. Over and over, I repeated, "I forgive you, Mom." It was difficult, but I knew it was the only way to get past it.

When I reached the top of the stairs, I took a left, walked down the hall, and ended up in my child-hood bedroom. Turning on the light, I looked around. So much of what formed me had happened in that room. I had spent countless nights curled up in my bed, crying into my pillow, trying to understand what was so fundamentally wrong with me that my own mother couldn't love me.

All my life had been spent trying to unravel the knotted-up strings of that question. If your own parents didn't want you, if they couldn't love you, how was it possible for anyone else to? How was it possible to even love yourself?

At the heart of it all, that had been my lifelong struggle—to love and accept myself. I knew I was still a long way from being there, but I was closer than I'd ever been. Forgiving my mother had been the first step. The only missing piece was Charlie's forgiveness, but I knew that wasn't possible. I was going to have to try to move on without it.

Taking a deep breath, I slowly arranged my painting supplies on the floor. The carpeting hadn't yet been replaced, so I didn't need to worry about spills or splatters. I stepped back and took a long look at the blank wall, letting all my feelings and emotions about the room settle. I plugged my phone into the outlet to charge, found my favorite radio station, took a deep breath, and dipped my brush into the paint.

———

THE SKY GREW DARK OUTSIDE THE LARGE window, but still I painted. I had made good progress on the mural, and I was basking in the healing power of leaving it all on my chosen canvas. I didn't know how much time had passed, but I didn't care. I painted on.

As I painted, my entire childhood danced through my mind. Memories surfaced, ones I had buried so deeply I thought they were forgotten. Images floated in my mind's eye, ones I'd rather not see, but I accepted each one for what it was—a real moment that shaped the person I'd become.

Sometimes I cried. Sometimes I smiled. I knew that true art was just an extension of the artist's emotions, so I let it all out. I channeled everything I felt into the painting. I experienced the hurt, as well as the acceptance of that pain, with every single brushstroke.

Glancing at my phone, I was shocked to discover that it was nearly six o'clock in the morning. I'd been painting for hours, literally all night long, although it felt like only minutes. I hadn't stopped to eat anything, only taking quick breaks to go to the bathroom when absolutely necessary.

I was beginning to feel a bit light-headed, so I reached into my purse and grabbed a granola bar. Ripping off the wrapper, I stuffed it into my mouth, then walked down the hall to wash it down with some water. After taking care of my overdue bathroom needs, I washed my hands and walked back toward my bedroom.

I was caught up in the euphoria of my creation, so I wasn't as aware of my surroundings as I probably should have been. I didn't see the giant brute of a man, dressed all in black, standing inside the bedroom until it was too late.

Stark fear froze me in place. I couldn't run. I couldn't do anything but stare at him, horror and confusion slowing my reflexes.

"Who are you? What are you doing in here?"

I forced my voice not to shake, trying not to convey the utter terror that gripped my gut.

"Hadley Monroe? That's you, right?" he barked.

"Who wants to know?"

I stiffened my back and looked around the room for something, anything, I could grab to defend myself. There was nothing.

"You've been hard to track down, but it looks like I finally found you."

"Found me? Why are you even looking for me?"

"Like you don't know," the man scoffed.

"I don't know. I have no idea why you would be tracking me down," I insisted, panic rising in my chest.

"You don't answer your phone. That's bad. You should pick up when people call you."

My mind raced, trying to figure out what he was talking about. Then I remembered all the random missed calls I'd received—phone calls with no voicemails. I also recalled the times I'd felt like I was being watched. Suddenly all the pieces came crashing together.

The man sneered, cracking his knuckles, as well as his neck, in a move that I'm sure was meant to intimidate me. It worked.

"What do you want from me?"

"The money," he sneered. "What else would I want?"

"I swear I don't know what you're talking about. I've never seen you before, and I certainly don't have your money."

I racked my brain, trying to understand who the man was and what he could possibly be talking about, but I came up empty.

"Borrowing money from a loan shark comes with certain—what's the word I'm looking for here— hazards. Especially if you don't repay and try to skip town."

He reached into his coat pocket and pulled out a sharp, shiny knife. Every cell in my body screamed out for me to run, but my feet felt as if they were encased in concrete.

"I've never borrowed money from a loan shark in my life," I cried. "You have the wrong person. I don't know what you're talking about. Please. Don't hurt me."

"Your husband borrowed money from my boss, and since he's not here to collect from, lady, it's up to you. That's how this works."

As he said the words, the shocking reality of the situation surfaced in my brain and screamed at me, an answer I didn't want to hear. I hadn't borrowed money from a loan shark, but Charlie had.

My husband's gambling problem apparently went even deeper than I'd realized. Not only had he triple mortgaged our home, spent all our savings, and racked up a load of credit card debt, he'd also borrowed cash from a loan shark—the mystery cash I'd been living off of for the past few months. I'd nearly spent it all, and the loan shark's goon was there to collect, one way or another.

"Look, I had no idea where that money came from. I didn't know. Please, don't hurt me. I'm a mother. I have daughters who need me. Please, you have to understand, Charlie is dead," I pleaded.

"Save it, lady. I've heard it all before. Your

husband borrowed the money; he didn't pay it back. I don't really care if he's dead. Now it's on you."

"Wait," I stalled. "How much money?"

"Forty thousand. Now, if you have that on you, you can hand it over and we'll call it good."

"Forty thousand dollars?" My voice cracked.

How could Charlie have borrowed forty thousand dollars in cash? The money I'd found in his drawer hadn't added up to even half of that, which meant he'd already spent the rest before I came across it. How could I have been so blind to his problems? How was it possible that I hadn't really known my husband at all?

I swallowed hard and tried to reason with the man. "Look, I don't have that much money."

"That's not my problem."

"I mean, I don't even know how soon I could get that much money," I said desperately. "I don't even have a job."

"That's what I thought. And my patience has run out. The time for talking is over."

The man started walking toward me, and I backed away, glancing behind me, praying for a way out. My feet finally came to life and I turned and ran, but I wasn't fast enough. In a couple of strides, the man's long legs easily caught up with me. He grabbed me by the hair and dragged me back into the bedroom.

Shoving me hard against the wall, he held me in place with one large beefy hand and punched me in the face with the other. My head snapped backwards, smashing against the wall. My mouth filled with the metallic taste of blood, and the room began to spin.

I tried to struggle, to break free of his grip, but he was much too strong. When I squirmed, he lifted his knee and rammed me in the middle. Then he slammed my body against the wall once more. I heard a crack, and I knew he'd broken ribs. Doubling over, my body slid like liquid to the floor. I curled into a ball, trying to protect my head as his large, booted foot kicked me over and over again.

As he made contact with my head, my last lucid thought was *this is how I die.*

CHAPTER TWENTY

MACK FINISHED BUTTERING THE TOAST. HE placed it on the plate and covered the bacon and eggs with some aluminum foil. He wanted to keep it hot. He filled a large travel mug with coffee, added a splash of cream, just the way she liked it, and placed the lid on top.

Grabbing some silverware and a napkin, he headed out his front door, walked across the lawn, and did his best to balance everything in one hand while he knocked on the door to Hadley's mother's house with the other.

He'd been worried about Hadley all night but wanted to give her space to do whatever it was she needed to do. Clearly it had been important to her. It was still quite early, but he felt like he'd waited long enough. He knocked a few more times, but she didn't answer. Maybe she had called one of the girls to come and pick her up. Or maybe she'd just fallen asleep.

He placed the food on the ground, dug around in his pocket, and fished out the house key. He unlocked the front door, grabbed the breakfast and coffee he'd made for Hadley, and stepped inside. The house was still and quiet.

"Hadley?" he called. "Are you here?"

His forehead wrinkled with confusion as he wondered where she could be. Quickly, he walked into the kitchen and placed the food and coffee on the countertop.

"Hadley?" he called again, that time a little louder, as he checked each of the rooms downstairs.

A prickle of worry crept up his spine as he headed toward the stairs. Climbing them two at a time, he scaled them quickly. He went down the hall that led to the master bedroom, checked the bathroom, and the second bedroom as well, but came up empty.

By that time, he was more than a little bit worried, so he picked up the pace and strode toward the third bedroom, the one Hadley said had belonged to her. Absolutely nothing could have prepared him for the gut punch he received when he saw her—the woman he loved—lying in a bloodied heap on the floor.

"Hadley!" he screamed as he ran into the room.

Mack dropped to his knees and reached for her wrist, gripping it desperately, hoping to find a pulse. He breathed a sigh of relief when he felt it, her slow, faint heartbeat. Trying to be gentle, he moved her body slightly, rolling her over so he could survey the damage.

Her face was beaten and bruised, distorted nearly beyond recognition. Her arms were cut. She was bleeding profusely, and none of it was crusted over, which told him it had happened recently. She'd clearly put up a good fight in an attempt to fend off whatever monster had attacked her.

As he continued his examination, he cursed out loud when he saw a knife sticking out of her side. The blood trickled, dripping steadily from the entrance wound. He resisted the impulse to pull it out, knowing it could spell disaster for her if it had punctured a vital organ. Instead, he grabbed his cell phone and dialed 911.

"911, what's your emergency?" asked the woman on the other end of the phone.

"I need an ambulance at 1223 Blackbird Lane.

The door is unlocked. Hurry, please hurry," he screamed, crying as he yelled the words into the phone.

"I'm dispatching emergency vehicles right now, sir," the woman replied efficiently, her steady voice oddly calming. "I'll stay on the line with you until they arrive."

Mack sat there, holding Hadley's broken body, praying harder than he'd ever prayed in his life. The 911 operator was still speaking, but he no longer had any idea what she was saying. He held Hadley's body and continued to pray, pleading with God not to take her away from him. He would give anything, anything at all, for her to be okay. He'd already lost one woman he loved, and he didn't know if he would be able to come back from losing another.

"Stay with me, Hadley, please," he begged. "Come on, baby, stay with me. Don't leave me now."

He didn't know how long he sat there, praying and holding her, but it felt like a lifetime. He could almost feel her slipping away from him as he waited for the ambulance. Finally, he heard them pounding on the door. Then he heard the knob turn, and the front door burst open.

Running footsteps pounded up the stairs as Mack yelled, "We're in here."

He didn't want to let go of her, but he reluctantly scooted away so the paramedics could do their jobs. "Please, help her. Please. She has to be okay."

"We'll do everything we can," one of them answered.

Mack stood to his feet and backed away, bracing his shaking legs and weary body against the wall, a million thoughts racing through his brain.

Who could have done this to her? How could this have happened? Why didn't I come over sooner?

If he hadn't waited so long, maybe he would have been there when she was attacked. Maybe she wouldn't have been attacked at all. The blood was fresh, which meant the attacker had been there recently. Maybe he had run off when he'd heard Mack come inside. If he'd been more observant, he would have caught the guy. If... maybe... none of it mattered. Nothing mattered but Hadley being okay.

"You can follow us in your car," the paramedic instructed Mack. He nodded numbly.

They worked quickly, gently lifting her body onto a stretcher. They braced her head and neck and rushed her down the stairs and outside into the waiting ambulance. Mack grabbed Hadley's purse and phone and started to follow them, but stopped dead in his tracks when he finally noticed the mural on the wall.

In that moment, he understood what had been so important, so crucial, for her to do. It was a mural of Hadley, Stella, and Celeste. The three of them were huddled together, clustered tightly, their bodies connected as if they were one single unit. She had captured herself and her daughters perfectly. They were standing in a meadow filled with wildflowers.

There was a huge crevasse at the end of the meadow, a rocky canyon that was sharp, jagged, and dangerous. On the other side of the crevasse stood a woman that Mack instantly recognized as Charlotte, Hadley's mom. But it wasn't the Charlotte he'd seen the night she died. This Charlotte was young, she was happy, and she was smiling. She was reaching her arms out toward her daughter and granddaughters, a look of hope on her lovely face. Colorful, abundant flowers grew out of her fingertips, intertwining, gathering together to form a sort of bridge that spanned across the crevasse leading to the meadow.

Mack understood exactly what Hadley was trying to convey. He knew that she had fully and completely forgiven her mother, and she'd felt the need to permanently commemorate an image of that forgiveness onto the wall of the bedroom in the house that had haunted her for years.

Mack knew that on the long, winding, broken road of her life, Hadley had finally found some peace.

CHAPTER TWENTY-ONE

THE AMBULANCE SPED TOWARD COTTAGE BROOK Community Hospital, Mack following closely in its wake. While he drove, he called Stella and Celeste, breaking the news as gently as he could, telling them they needed to get to the hospital right away. He heard the horror and fear in their voices, and he assured them he would be there waiting for them when they arrived.

He hung up and made a nearly identical phone call to Vivian. In typical Viv fashion, she informed him that she would be making a phone call of her own to the hospital to ensure Hadley would receive the best care possible, sparing no expense.

"I will call in the best specialists around, Mack.

She *will* be okay. She has to be," Vivian added, a slight quiver in her voice.

"I'm counting on it, Vivian," Mack said, his own voice breaking completely as he hung up the phone.

The ambulance pulled directly in front of the emergency room doors, and Mack wheeled into the parking lot. Zipping his truck into the nearest space, he parked it quickly and ran into the building. The paramedics whisked Hadley's gurney through the swinging double doors. They closed them behind her, and Mack felt stranded, isolated, cut off from the woman he'd come to love more than life itself.

"I'm here with Hadley Monroe," Mack said quickly to the woman behind the desk.

"Are you family?" she asked, tapping her pen on the counter.

"Well—er—no—I'm not—exactly family," he stammered.

"Then you'll need to go to the waiting room. Does she have family coming?"

"Yes, her daughters will be here soon."

"All information will need to go through them," the woman replied, scribbling something into a chart.

"But—" Mack interrupted.

"I'm sorry, sir, it's hospital procedure," the

woman replied. "Please take a seat in the waiting room."

Deflated and helpless, Mack sank into a waiting room chair. No, he wasn't technically her family, but he sure felt like it. He loved Hadley with a protective ferocity that nearly took his breath away, and to be kept away from her was almost more than he could take. She had to be all right. She had to be.

He glanced up and saw the terrified faces of Stella and Celeste as the girls ran through the emergency room doors. Rising quickly, he met them at the entrance, where both girls nearly collapsed into his arms.

"Where is she? Is she going to be okay?" Stella sobbed.

"What happened to her?" Celeste asked.

"I don't know. I found her on the floor of your grandmother's house this morning when I took her breakfast. She was hurt pretty badly, but I have no idea what happened. When I left her there yesterday, she was fine. And I didn't want to bother her," he said helplessly, wishing he had a better explanation. "I called the ambulance and followed them here."

"Have they said anything since she arrived?" Stella asked, her eyes wide with fear.

"They won't tell me. I'm not family," Mack replied, his eyes welling up with tears.

"Yes, you are, Mack," Stella said as she hugged him tightly.

"Well, I'm family, and I'm going to find out what's going on," Celeste declared, raising her chin defiantly as she approached the front desk. "My name is Celeste Monroe, and my mother, Hadley Monroe, was just brought in. I would like an update on her condition immediately."

"Of course, Ms. Monroe. Please have a seat and the doctor will be right out," the receptionist replied.

Mack, Stella, and Celeste formed a small huddle in the waiting room area. After what seemed like an interminably long time, a man approached them.

"Are you here for Hadley Monroe?" he asked. "I'm Dr. Novak."

"Yes, we are. She's our mother," Stella said, gripping Celeste's hand in her own.

"Is she going to be okay? What's wrong with her?" Celeste asked.

"Your mother has been hurt quite badly. She has multiple issues that we're trying to get under control. We're doing our best to get her stabilized right now. Are you the ones who found her?" Dr. Novak inquired.

"No, I am," Mack chimed in. "I live next door to Hadley's mother's house, and I knew she was there. When I didn't hear from her, I went to check in on her, and I found her... like... that. I called 911...."

"I see. Her injuries are severe. Do you know of anyone who would want to hurt her?" Dr. Novak asked. "I see a lot of terrible things, working in an ER. The police generally say that attacks like this are personal."

"No, I have no idea why anyone would want to hurt Hadley. And it's a good thing I don't, because if I knew who did this to her, I'd rip them apart with my bare hands," Mack gritted out through his teeth.

Dr. Novak's face softened. "I'm sorry. It must have been difficult to find her that way."

"You can't even imagine," Mack replied, his eyes glistening with tears.

"So, we have no idea what happened to her then?" Stella asked, her voice quivering.

"We don't. But judging from the way she was beaten, and the fact that someone stabbed her, whoever attacked her didn't seem to care if she made it out alive. And they nearly succeeded," Dr. Novak explained. "The good news is that the injuries are recent, meaning they happened shortly before she was brought in. That works in her favor, because otherwise, she may have bled out."

"She was stabbed?" Celeste gasped, her hands flying up to cover her mouth. "Who would do that to her?"

"The police are going to do their best to find that out. The detectives have already arrived. They've taken the knife into evidence, and they'll be dusting it for fingerprints. My guess is that this person was an amateur. It was really stupid of them to leave that knife behind, but it will certainly be helpful in finding them. It was a crucial mistake. The detectives will need to take a look at the crime scene, and I'm sure they'll have a lot of questions for all of you," Dr. Novak said.

"We'll answer whatever they need to know. They have to find whoever did this to our mom," Stella replied.

"What all is wrong with her? Is she awake? Can we see her?" Celeste asked.

"Ms. Monroe, your mother is in a coma right now. She's been unresponsive since she arrived. She has multiple broken ribs, a broken arm, a body full of lacerations, and a fractured skull. The stab wound was quite deep, so we need to watch for infection, but it looks like no permanent organ damage was done. She has a long road ahead of her, and right now, we need to take it a minute at a time. We have to wait it out and hope she regains consciousness soon," the doctor explained gently.

"A coma? That's really bad," Mack breathed.

"It can be. Or not. At this point, it's really too soon to tell. The prognosis varies from patient to patient, and her chances of recovery depend on a lot of factors, including how long it takes her to wake up. I wish I could give you something definite to hold on to, but I'm afraid that's just not possible right now," Dr. Novak said. "I will tell you that she is in very good hands, and we are doing everything we can for her."

"Can we see her?" Stella asked.

"She's in intensive care. You can see her in shifts. I don't want to overwhelm her, and I want the doctors and nurses to be able to do their jobs right now. But you can go in one at a time."

"What about me? Can I go in?" Mack asked, already knowing the answer.

"Are you a member of her family?" Dr. Novak inquired.

"I'm—" Mack began.

"He's my mother's fiancé. Of course, he's family," Stella interrupted, meeting Mack's eyes.

"Then if that's the case, yes, you may see her. Give us a bit of time and I'll send a nurse out to let one of you come back soon," the doctor replied before walking away.

"Thank you, Stella," Mack said when the doctor was out of earshot. "I appreciate that. I need to see her."

"Mom would want you back there. I'm sure of it. I had to tell them something. I knew they wouldn't let you go otherwise." Stella shrugged.

"Thank you for understanding. I'm going to go grab some coffee while we wait. Can I get you girls something?"

"Coffee for both of us, too. It's going to be a long day," Celeste answered, pulling Stella into her arms.

CHAPTER TWENTY-TWO

I STOOD AT THE KITCHEN SINK, SCRUBBING THE pan as hard as I could. No matter how hard I scoured it, the stain wouldn't come out. The food was stuck, burned to the bottom, and no amount of elbow grease was going to lift it. Sighing, I let the water get hot and squirted some dish soap into the pan. It was going to have to soak a little longer.

I went to the counter and tossed the salad, drizzling vinaigrette onto the green leaves and adding some freshly ground pepper. Dinner was almost ready, but Charlie still wasn't home. Glancing at the clock on the stove, I wondered if he was going to be late again. That had become a habit of his lately.

Suddenly, I looked around the room and realized the kitchen was spinning, tilting on its side. The room was there, and then it wasn't; familiar, then foreign. Grabbing the countertop to steady myself, I tried to figure out what was happening. All at once my head snapped back, and I tasted the metallic flavor of blood in my mouth. Then I heard my ribs crack. What was happening?

The room was spinning out of control. My ears were ringing, but then the sound cleared. In its place, I heard a strange, steady beeping sound in the background, almost like a hospital monitor. Where was I? Where was Charlie? Why was he late for dinner again? There was something he wasn't telling me.

Charlie...

His name spiked some elusive memory, just beyond my grasp. Charlie and I were fighting. He was angry. He stormed out of the house. I said something terrible. I hurt him. He'd never forgive me.

Charlie... Charlie... Charlie...

In a flash of light, it all came back to me.

"Fine! Yes, I am having an affair, Charlie. I'm in love with another man. Is that what you want to hear?" I screamed at him, the rage seething, tearing me in two, ripping through my body.

Why was I so angry?

Charlie...

Charlie's head jerked up and he looked at me, his

face falling, crumpling like a wadded-up sheet of paper as the impact of my words hit him head-on.

Head-on—just like the bus that killed him.

Charlie... Charlie... don't leave... don't walk out the door...

His eyes filled with tears and his body shook with anger. He stared at me for a couple of minutes, then he stalked away. His footsteps echoed through the house as he stomped into the kitchen, grabbed his car keys, and slammed the front door.

I heard his car start in the driveway; the hum of the motor inordinately loud in the quiet of the room. The car's engine revved, and the tires spun, spitting gravel as he sped away from the house.

"Fine, go!" I screamed at the door. "I don't want you here anyway!"

My hands trembled, and my insides twisted as the realization of what I'd done settled in on me. I'd told Charlie I loved someone else. I'd told him I was having an affair. But I wasn't. Why had I said it? I wanted to take it back.

Charlie... Charlie...

"Good. That's what he deserves. He shouldn't accuse me of things I haven't done," I insisted, speaking to the walls. "Let him stew on that for a while. Maybe now he'll tell me why he's been so distant with me lately."

Yes, sometimes the only way to fix things was to stir the pot a little. Charlie and I had been stagnant for so long that I felt like I was drowning in the still waters. I needed to make some waves, to roil the silt at the bottom of the lake and see what came up. Charlie and I needed to agitate the waters of our marriage, then let it settle and see if we could still float.

"Everything is going to be just fine. He'll calm down and then we can talk about all of it. This will be good for us," I convinced myself as I went to make dinner.

Once again, I was in the kitchen, tossing the salad, drizzling vinaigrette onto the leaves and sprinkling them with ground pepper when I heard the knock at the door. The sight of the policeman standing on my doorstep told me that my wishful thinking was just that. Things between Charlie and me would never be fine again.

Charlie...

The bus hit him head-on, Mrs. Monroe...

Charlie... come back...

He was killed on impact, Mrs. Monroe...

Charlie... don't go...

"No!" I cried, pounding the policeman's chest with my fists. "He can't be dead. He'll never know the truth now."

I crumpled to the floor and screamed at the top of my lungs. "Please, Charlie, please don't be dead. Please come back. You have to know the truth."

The pain was too much, and the room went black. I cried in the darkness for a thousand years. But then the space was no longer dark. In fact, I shielded my eyes as a blinding light ripped through the room.

"Hadley, honey, why are you crying?"

Charlie's soothing voice was like music to my ears.

"Charlie?" I asked, disoriented. "How are you here? They said you were dead."

"I am." Reaching his hand toward me, Charlie helped me to my feet.

"If you're dead—then how—does that mean I'm —dead too?" I asked.

"Not exactly. You're somewhere in between, honey," Charlie answered with a smile.

"How can that be?"

"I don't really know how this all works." He shrugged, grinning that Charlie grin that won me over all those years ago.

My heart exploded with love for him, and I never wanted to let him go. I was there, wherever it was, with Charlie, and everything was going to be okay.

"I'm so glad to see you." I threw my arms around him, holding him as tightly as I could. "I'm never letting go of you. I've missed you so much."

"I know. I've missed you too."

"So, I can stay here? With you?" I asked.

"Is that really what you want? What about our daughters? They need you."

"Stella and Celeste," I murmured, picturing their faces.

"And what about Mack?" Charlie raised one very astute eyebrow at me.

"Mack? You know about Mack?" I asked, my stomach flipping.

"I know enough," he replied.

"Then you know I lied to you? Oh, Charlie, I lied to you that day. I told you I had an affair, and it was a lie. I wanted to hurt you," I gushed, spewing out the words I'd wanted to say for so long.

"You did hurt me," Charlie admitted. "But I hurt you, too."

"Yes, you did. Oh, Charlie, you weren't honest with me either, were you?"

"I wasn't. I was ashamed. My gambling was out

of control, and I was ashamed. I should have told you. If I had turned to you instead of away from you, maybe none of this would have happened," he shrugged. "I'm so sorry, Hadley."

"I know, Charlie, I know," I said as I held him close, stroking my hands across his back to soothe him. He'd always liked it when I did that. "I'm sorry too."

"I forgive you," he answered, and the sound was like music to my ears.

"And I forgive you." I pulled him closer, never wanting to let go. "Can we just stay like this? Forever?"

"I don't think so, Hadley."

"But why not? Why do I have to leave you?"

"Because you're not done yet." He pulled away from me. "Tell Stella and Celeste that I love them so much."

"But, Charlie—"

I reached out for him, but he kept getting farther and farther away from me.

"There's so much left for you to do. All those years you waited—afraid, guilty—now's your chance, Hadley. It's time for you to really live. You don't have to be scared anymore. Please don't be afraid."

He was drifting away, and before long, he would be gone altogether.

"Charlie—wait!" I called, desperate for him to hear me. "I love you."

"I love you too, honey. I've loved you since the first day I saw you, spilling that food all over the sidewalk." Charlie laughed, his voice growing more distant.

"I can't see you, Charlie," I called, hungry for another second with him.

"But I can see you, Hadley. All those years you thought you were invisible, but you never were. Not to me. I see you, honey. I've always seen you."

"Charlie—" I called, spinning in circles, desperately trying to find him, but it was no use.

Charlie was gone.

CHAPTER TWENTY-THREE

I blinked my eyes several times, then closed them quickly, the blinding light of the room too much to take in. Everything was too bright, too loud, too much.

"Mom!" Stella cried. "Mom, can you hear me? Help! Somebody! She's awake!"

The room came alive with people buzzing here and there. Monitors beeped, nurses poked and prodded me, and the overall energy in the room kicked up about a hundred notches.

"Hadley, I'm Dr. Novak," a man said. "Welcome back."

"Back?"

I tried to speak, but my throat felt like sandpaper. It came out as more of a groan.

"She's awake?" Celeste called as she ran into the room.

"She is," Stella answered, the sound of tears in her sweet voice.

"How long—" I tried again.

"You've been in a coma for five days, Hadley. You've had us all pretty worried," Dr. Novak replied as he shone a bright light in my eyes.

"Water—" I croaked.

A nurse came to my side and adjusted the pillows on my bed, gently helping me to settle into a semi-upright position. I grimaced and blew out a painful breath. I was fully awake, and everything hurt. I greedily sipped the water she held out for me.

"Not too fast," the nurse warned, pulling it away from my lips and placing it on the bedside tray.

"What happened to me?" I asked.

I glanced around the room, trying to adjust myself to the surroundings. I was clearly in a hospital room, and from the way my body felt, I was injured pretty badly. I looked at my daughters' faces, tear-streaked and happy. I took in the expectant face of the nurse and the serious face of Dr. Novak.

Finally, my eyes settled on the large figure in the corner of the room.

"Mack," I breathed, my eyes filling with tears when I saw him. "You're here."

I tried to smile, but it hurt too badly. He wiped the tears that flowed freely down his cheeks and smiled back at me.

"I told you I wasn't going anywhere," he said quietly.

"Mack has been here every single day, Mom. He's barely left your side," Stella answered, squeezing my hand gently.

"That man really cares about you, Mama," Celeste chimed in, leaning down to kiss my forehead. Then she whispered in my ear, "Don't mess it up."

"I don't plan to," I whispered back.

I cringed a little as I tried to sit up a bit more in the bed. Celeste bent down and helped adjust the pillows behind me. Once I was settled, I cleared my throat, hoping my voice would hold out for what I had to say.

"Stella, Celeste, I want you to know that your dad loves you. He told me to tell you that he loves you both very much."

"Dad? What do you mean?" Stella asked, her chin quivering.

"You saw Dad?" Celeste's eyes, so much like Charlie's, filled with tears.

"I did, yeah, I did. As far-fetched as it sounds, I saw your dad. And I can't really explain it. But he wanted me to tell you both that he loves you." I relayed Charlie's message to his daughters.

The girls looked at each other and smiled through their tears, pulling each other close. I knew it was exactly what they needed to hear. His passing had been so sudden, and they'd never gotten the chance to say goodbye.

"I can't believe you're awake, Mom," Celeste said. "And you saw Dad."

"This is the best day ever," Stella added. "And I'm starving. We're going to get some food. I haven't been able to eat for five days, but now that you're awake, I want to eat everything in sight."

"Go eat. I'm not going anywhere," I replied with the best smile I could muster.

My daughters joined hands and walked out of the room together. The nurse followed them.

"I'll be back in a bit to check on you. You need to rest. You're awake, but you still have a long recovery ahead of you," Dr. Novak warned.

"Thank you, Doctor," I answered.

Then the room was empty except for me and Mack.

He hadn't moved from the corner, and I just sat

there looking at him while a thousand thoughts and emotions swirled around inside of me. I had known for a while that I was in love with him, but the moment had never seemed right to admit my feelings. Now I understood what I'd been waiting for—Charlie's forgiveness.

Somehow, although I still didn't quite understand the details, I'd been given the chance to work things out with Charlie. We'd admitted our faults, and we'd forgiven each other. Although it hadn't happened in the way I'd wanted, getting the chance to see him again, to feel him, to talk to him, was the most amazing, unexpected gift. He'd given me his blessing.

I finally knew without a shadow of a doubt that Charlie wanted me to be happy. And one of the keys to my happiness was standing in the corner of my hospital room.

"Hadley," Mack began as he approached the hospital bed. "I'm so glad you're awake."

"Me too." I patted the bed beside me, indicating that he should sit down.

"I don't want to hurt you." He hesitated.

"You won't," I answered, patting the bed again. "I'm sure of it."

He gently sat on the mattress, careful not to

jostle my still-fragile body. Tentatively, he reached out and grabbed my hand.

"I thought I'd lost you. When I found you like that—" he started but couldn't seem to finish.

"You're the one who found me?"

"Yes. It was the absolute worst moment of my life. I've never felt more helpless." His eyes glistened with tears.

"I still don't remember everything, but it's slowly coming back to me," I stated. "Did they catch the guy?"

"Yeah, they did. They ran the fingerprints on the knife. He was pretty stupid not to use gloves," Mack said angrily.

"I don't think he meant to stab me. I think the knife was just to scare me. I don't think he expected me to fight back at all. I think he was just going to beat me up, but then someone knocked on the door downstairs and he panicked and ran. It seemed like stabbing me was a spur-of-the-moment decision on his part," I said, the events slowly trickling back into my brain.

"That was me knocking on the door. I just missed him. I'd have loved to get my hands on him," Mack said through gritted teeth. "You didn't know him, did you?"

"No. But Charlie did." I sighed.

"What?" Mack asked, shock registering on his face.

"After Charlie died, I found out that he had a pretty bad gambling problem. He basically left us with nothing but a giant pile of debt. Apparently, he'd borrowed cash from a loan shark, and when he didn't pay them back, they came after me instead."

"Hadley—" Anger flashed in Mack's eyes.

"Charlie was a good man, Mack. He was a great father and husband. He made a mistake. He would never have wanted me to get hurt," I explained, feeling a fierce protectiveness for my husband.

"I'm sure he wouldn't have. But you did get hurt," Mack stated matter-of-factly.

"I did. But I also hurt him, Mack. I hurt him in a way that I couldn't take back, and the guilt that followed me around after his death was almost more than I could bear," I said, trying to find the right words to explain.

"What did you do?" Mack asked. "I'm sorry, that's none of my business. It has nothing to do with me."

"Actually, it does," I answered.

"How is that possible?"

"Charlie and I were having problems. He was

distant, secretive. It went on for months. We grew farther and farther apart until we barely talked at all. I was hungry for connection. I felt like Charlie couldn't see me anymore. I felt like I had become invisible. About that time, I met you in the coffee shop," I began.

"I see." Mack's forehead wrinkled.

"The connection between us, well, you know how it was. It was like nothing I'd ever felt before. I went back to that coffee shop every day for a month, just hoping to run into you again, to feel the way I'd felt when I was with you. To have someone see me."

"I didn't know that."

"I tried my hardest to forget about you, to forget that amazing afternoon I had with you. But I couldn't. No matter what I did, I couldn't stop thinking about you, Mack. Eventually, Charlie noticed. He accused me of having an affair. At first, I denied it. I kept trying to forget about you, but it was no use. The day he died, he accused me again of having an affair, and something inside of me exploded. I admitted to it," I explained.

"But you hadn't done anything," Mack said, confusion on his face.

"Don't you see? I felt so guilty about my feelings for you that I believed I needed to be punished. I also wanted to punish Charlie, to make him feel bad to make myself feel better," I tried to explain. "Ugh, I know that none of this probably makes any sense to you."

"You were angry at him for shutting you out," Mack replied, understanding dawning.

"Yes. Charlie left the house, madder than I'd ever seen him, and two miles down the road he crashed his car. He died that day, never knowing the truth."

"And you've carried around the guilt," Mack said, the lightbulb going off in his brain.

"So much guilt. And then with everything that happened with my mother, well, when I came to Cottage Brook, I was basically hell-bent on punishing myself for the rest of my life."

"And then..." Mack trailed off.

"And then I opened my mother's door, and there you were. All of a sudden, everything clicked into place and scattered into a million pieces at the same time. I had no idea what to do with any of it."

"I understand now. It all makes sense," Mack said quietly, nodding his head.

"But when I was—in—the coma—" I tried to organize my words, but they jumbled up inside my head.

"It's okay, Hadley, you don't have to explain," Mack assured me.

"I want to," I said. "When I was in the coma, Mack, I saw Charlie. I finally got the one thing I needed in order to move on."

"What was that?"

"Forgiveness. Charlie forgave me, and I got the chance to do the same for him."

"All of this happened while you were—out?" Mack asked.

"It did. And I know it doesn't make any sense, but it was just what I needed in order to do what I have to do next."

I swallowed hard, my heart rate increasing, as evidenced by the monitor beeping beside me.

"What do you have to do?"

Mack squeezed my hand a little tighter.

"I have to tell you how I really feel about you."

I looked into the blue eyes that had captured me, heart and soul, that fateful day in the coffee shop.

"I already know how you feel." He smiled. "We're friends, right?"

"Oh, Mack, you know me better than that. You've known all along how I feel. I'm the one who's had a hard time coming around to it."

"And exactly how do you feel, Hadley?"

He inched a little closer to me. The monitor beeped even faster.

"I am in love with you." I gulped as I said the words. "So very much in love with you, Mack Kinley."

"It's about time." He laughed. "Because I'm head over heels in love with you too."

He gently took my face into his hands and glided his thumb across the bruises on my cheek. Moving in closer, he paused, looking at me, drinking me in, seeing me more clearly than anyone in the whole world ever had.

Not able to wait another second, I closed the gap between us and brushed my lips against his as the hospital room exploded with fireworks.

CHAPTER TWENTY-FOUR

IT WAS ANOTHER THREE WEEKS BEFORE I WAS discharged from the hospital, and even then, I was still not running on all cylinders. Miraculously, I had no long-term side effects from the fractured skull, and my broken arm was healing nicely. The ribs were still painful, and my stab wound had become infected, forcing me to spend an extra week in the hospital in order to get things under control. The laceration was still tender, but I was on the road to recovery.

My attacker would go to trial, with the possibility of being sentenced to twenty-five years in prison. The detectives had linked him to other cases, and the attorneys had been able to tack on a few other charges. Aunt Viv had paid off Charlie's outstanding debt to the loan shark, so my slate was clean. I had nothing to fear from loan sharks anymore.

Celeste and Stella put our Cleveland house on the market, and it had sold almost immediately. Viv had hired movers, and my former home was ready for its next owners. All the decisions that had weighed me down for months had been taken care of by those who loved me the most. I hadn't needed to shoulder the burden alone after all. All I'd needed to do was ask for help. It had been there waiting all the time.

That morning, Mack had driven me to Cleveland, and after tying up some loose ends, we were in his Camaro, headed back to Cottage Brook. The girls had gone to Cleveland as well, but they were staying a few extra days in order to say goodbye to their friends before making their permanent moves to Cottage Brook.

Celeste had decided to quit her job. She was sad to leave, but my hospital stay convinced her that she wanted to be close by me and her sister. She had received a stellar recommendation from her boss, and already had a job lined up at the hospital lab in Cottage Brook.

I had bid farewell to the home that sheltered my family for the better part of my life. I knew it was time to let it go, but it was heart-wrenching to do so. Mack and my daughters had seen me through it, just as they'd seen me through everything that had come my way the past few months. I had a strong support system, and I knew my little family was going to be just fine.

Mack had finished the remodel on my mother's house, and it was lovely. He had managed to banish all the shadows lurking in the corners, filling the home with light and love. In a move that shocked even me, I had gifted the house to my daughters, leaving the decision to them about whether or not it stayed in the family. If they wanted to keep it, that was up to them. If they wanted to sell it, they had my blessing. The girls agreed that I would live there until I got my life all figured out.

To say that we had been on an emotional roller coaster would be the understatement of the year.

"How are you doing?" Mack turned toward me, a look of concern on his face. "Are you in any pain?"

"I'm fine." I smiled, reaching over to hold his hand. "And I really mean it this time."

"Are you up for one more stop when we get back into town?" Mack asked.

"I think I can handle that," I answered. "Where are we going?"

"It's a surprise," he answered cryptically.

I smiled to myself, wondering what he had up his sleeve.

We drove through town, past the hotel, all the way down Main Street, and finally turned right onto Stark Street, in the upscale area of Cottage Brook. Mack pulled the car into a parking space, turned it off, and came around to my side to help me out.

"Where are we?" I asked, a bit confused.

"You'll see."

He led me to a storefront and slipped a key into the door. Flipping on the lights, I smiled when I saw how lovely the space was. It had high ceilings, lined with decorative track lighting, as well as a few skylights. The newly polished hardwood floors gleamed. Stepping fully inside the room, I gasped in shock.

My paintings lined the walls of the room, both the ones I'd painted recently, as well as all the ones that hung on the walls of my home in Cleveland.

"What's this?" I breathed, walking slowly around the room, lightly touching each piece of artwork.

"This is your gallery," Mack answered, his face beaming with joy.

"My gallery? I don't understand."

"Your aunt Viv has owned this space for years.

She and I have discussed different options for it for some time. She had a lot of ideas that never panned out, and all this beautiful space has just been sitting here, empty," Mack began as he walked across the room toward me.

My heart beat wildly as I took in his words. Butterflies beat their wings inside my stomach, and I wiped my sweaty palms on my jeans. I didn't know why I was so nervous, but something told me I was standing on a precipice, just waiting to jump into the rest of my life.

"When I saw your paintings, Hadley, I immediately thought of this space. I knew it would be the perfect spot for an art gallery. I talked to Viv and the girls about it, and we all felt the same way—we wanted to make it happen for you."

"You were all in on it together?"

My heart beat a little faster as I realized that the place was all mine—my gallery.

"Yep. Your daughters gathered up all the paintings from your house in Cleveland while you were in the hospital, and we added the ones you'd done recently. I sent in a crew to spruce the place up a bit, and here we are. Your gallery."

He spread his arms wide and gestured around

the room, a look of both pleasure and pride on his handsome face.

"It's all mine," I whispered, attempting to take it all in. "It's like a dream come true."

"It's yours. You can paint in the back room—I have it all fixed up for you with all your supplies—and you can display and sell your own art, as well as other artists you come across. Cottage Brook could use a little culture, and you're just the person for the job."

"I can't believe it. I—I don't even know what to say."

I was truly at a loss for words. Mack and my family had believed in me long before I'd ever believed in myself. They understood my dreams, and they not only encouraged them, they were helping me reach out and grab them.

In a bit of a daze, I took another lap around my very own gallery, soaking it all in.

"I'll put a glass case on that wall over there," I pointed, my excitement growing. "To display Stella's jewelry."

"Great idea," Mack agreed.

"And I plan to seek out local artists, the undiscovered ones who need someone to believe in them and their work. I'm going to fill this room with art, Mack," I said excitedly, turning around to face him.

As if there hadn't already been enough surprises for the evening, Mack had one more. There he was, down on one knee, reaching up to take my hand in his.

"What—what—are you doing?" I stammered.

"Hadley Monroe, I've been waiting to make you mine since the first day I laid eyes on you, way back in the coffee shop that day. It's been a bit of a winding road that's brought us to this point, but that's exactly how I know it's right. Fate brought us together that day, and it has been working to bring us together every day since then."

Mack swallowed hard. Without ever breaking eye contact, he released my hand, reached into his pocket, and pulled out a small red velvet box. As he opened it, I noticed his hands were shaking, and it just made me love him all the more. A beautiful diamond ring was nestled inside.

"You would make me the happiest man in the world if you would be my wife," he said, his voice shaking with emotion. "Hadley, will you marry me?"

I hesitated, not because I was uncertain, but because I wanted to bask in the moment, to hold it in my mind forever, to really feel what I was feeling. I knew it was a moment I would never forget.

With tears rolling down my face, I nodded.

"Yes, Mack. A million times yes."

He stood to his feet and took me in his arms. Pulling me close, he slowly lowered his face to mine. As our lips met, we made a thousand promises to each other—promises I knew we would keep forever.

EPILOGUE

I took a deep breath and walked into my gallery. Taking a second to smooth down my wedding gown, I smiled, settling into the moment.

"Are you ready, Mom?" Stella asked as she threaded her right arm through my left one.

"I am so ready," I answered, tears glistening in my eyes.

"You look beautiful. Let's do this," Celeste said as she linked her left arm with my right.

With my daughters on either side of me, we walked down the aisle runner we had placed in the middle of the gallery floor. The room was filled with friends and family who wanted to share in our special day. Mack and I hadn't wanted an elaborate wedding, but we definitely wanted to make it memorable.

Rather than a church ceremony, I wanted to marry Mack in my gallery, the space that he had helped make possible for me to follow my dreams. I wanted to promise my life to him surrounded by my art, my family, and all those who loved us. I couldn't think of a more perfect way to begin our future.

As I walked toward Mack, standing there in his tux, looking better than any man had the right to, I went through the old wedding rhyme in my head, checking off all the boxes, making sure I hadn't forgotten anything.

Something old, something new, something borrowed, something blue.

I knew it was a silly superstition, but I wasn't taking any chances. For my something old, I was wearing Aunt Viv's wedding dress. She had actually cried when I'd asked her if I could wear it. Of course, she denied that she was crying, and insisted it was just her allergies acting up. I knew better, though. Viv never had a daughter to pass it down to, and she had always been like a mother to me, so wearing it felt right. In typical Viv fashion, she called in a fancy designer who restructured the gown, modernizing it a bit and tailoring it to my own personal style. It was absolutely perfect.

For my something new, Stella had made me a beautiful pearl necklace that accentuated the neckline of the gown. For the something borrowed, Celeste loaned me the diamond earrings that Charlie had bought her for her high school graduation.

And finally, for the something blue, I had asked the designer to incorporate a piece of the fabric from the blue shirt that I'd been wearing that day in the coffee shop when I met Mack. After all, that seemingly unremarkable shirt was what set this entire thing in motion in the first place.

The date of the wedding had been chosen with care—exactly two years from the day that Mack and I first met. As I thought back on that time, I couldn't believe the ways in which my life had changed.

Had I known that day in the coffee shop that the conversation I was about to have would forever alter the course of my life, I don't think I would have believed it. If I could have seen into the future, far down the road to how it would all end, I would have understood that everything that happened was Fate —exactly the way it was supposed to be.

They say hindsight is 20/20, and I believed that more than ever before.

That conversation between Mack and me, that one brief moment in time, that small blip on the radar of my life, sparked the incessant questions that awakened me from the dreamlike state in which I'd existed. I realized that I had always needed to ask myself those questions, no matter how painful the answers.

I had lived so much of my life in fear, so worried about staying inside my own small world, continuing to take up as little space as possible, afraid of reaching too high for fear of rocking the boat. I had nearly missed out on all the wonderful things that were waiting for me just beyond my grasp. They were there all along, I just had to take them.

On that ordinary Tuesday in October, two years earlier, Mack Kinley had stepped in line behind me at that coffee shop and commented on my shirt. The shirt was nothing special, just a blue blouse that I had worn a hundred times. It was completely unremarkable. Yet he remarked on it. He'd seen me when it felt like no one else had. He'd reminded me that I wasn't invisible. He'd upended my world and sent me on a path that turned out to be anything but ordinary.

Every second with him was magic. He made me feel like I was the only person in the room. He made me feel important, like I mattered. My life before Mack felt like a dress rehearsal for what was coming next. Mack made me better. He gave me the freedom to be fearless. When I met him, I had been so worried, always burdened with guilt, but he taught me how to let it go. Ever since the day I realized I loved him, I hadn't looked back for a second. I never wanted to leave the safety of that love.

Stella, Celeste, and I reached the end of the aisle. They both kissed me on each cheek, handed me over to Mack, and took their places to the left of us. Mack took my hands inside of his, then brought one of them up to his lips and kissed it.

The minister cleared his throat and began to speak. "In the Bible, in the book of Song of Solomon, we learn about love. We hear the words, 'I am my beloved's and my beloved is mine.' We read that 'many waters cannot quench love; rivers cannot wash it away.' And most importantly, we hear the phrase, 'I have found the one whom my soul loves.' We come together today to celebrate the love of Hadley and Mack, two souls who have proven that true love always finds one another in the end."

I glanced around the room at the people who were sharing the day with us. Aunt Viv smiled at me from her place in the front row, and I was pretty sure I even saw a few uncharacteristic tears in her eyes. I turned to the left and saw my daughters, arms wrapped around each other's waist, openly crying as they watched me join my life with Mack's.

I turned back toward Mack and smiled. When I did, I glanced behind him, at the far corner of the gallery. There stood Charlie, with his arm around my mother's shoulder. The two of them were beaming at me, and the love I felt from them nearly knocked me off my feet.

"I love you, honey," Charlie mouthed to me.

"I love you, too," I whispered, tears running down my cheeks. "I'll always love you."

The minister continued, "Do you Mack, take Hadley to be your wedded wife? To have and to hold from this day forward, for better, for worse, for richer, for poorer, in sickness and in health, to love and to cherish, till death do you part?"

"I do," Mack said, his voice ringing out loud and clear.

The minister repeated the same words to me, and I wholeheartedly agreed to the terms and conditions. Then he said, "I now pronounce you husband and wife. You may kiss the bride," and everything else faded away except the sensation of Mack's lips on mine.

"Looks like we made it," Mack whispered when we came up for air.

"We sure did," I answered with a smile.

"I never doubted it for a second," he added with a grin.

Sometimes I wondered if things might have turned out differently, if maybe Charlie would still be alive if I had handled things another way. I supposed I would never really know for sure. Maybe it all turned out exactly how it was meant to.

When it came right down to it, I really believed that was the truth. I often thought back to Charlie and the surreal moment I shared with him when I was trapped somewhere between life and death. That time with him was a gift I would always treasure.

No matter what, I would always love Charlie Monroe. He saved me in a thousand different ways. He was my husband, my lover, my surrogate father, and my friend. He was an amazing, dedicated father to our children. I lived my life with him longer than I lived it without him. I had no regrets about our marriage, other than our lack of truth with each other when it really mattered. Charlie would always own a very large chunk of my heart.

But I knew my future belonged to Mack. It's something I was sure of. His was the first face I wanted to see when I woke up in the morning, and it was the last one I wanted to look at before I went to sleep—every night for the rest of my life. I wanted to hold his hand forever, and when we were old and grey, I wanted to sit on our porch swing and talk about the beautiful life we built together.

I had come a long way in the last two years, since that day in the coffee shop. I felt like I was finally living the life I was intended to live. I was following my dreams, fulfilling my passions, and feeling my feelings.

But here's the most important thing of all—I had finally accepted myself, with all my flaws and imperfections, every bruise and insecurity. I was proud of the woman I had become, knowing how long it took me to get there. I knew that I was the kind of woman who deserved everything that came her way after that ordinary day.

I HOPE YOU ENJOYED THE SWEET ESCAPISM OF
FINDING THE INVISIBLE WOMAN. If you're looking
for a similar title from me, check out **ALWAYS HOPE**.
You may also love something with a fabulous mix of
humour and mystery that can be found in **LOVE AT
FIRST CREPE**.

ACKNOWLEDGMENTS

Thanks to everyone at Hot Tree Publishing for your amazing support of my work. Thank you for helping me bring *Finding the Invisible Woman* to life.

ABOUT THE AUTHOR

Thanks for reading *Finding the Invisible Woman*. I do hope you enjoyed my story. I appreciate your help in spreading the word, including telling a friend. Before you go, it would mean so much to me if you would take a few minutes to write a review and share how you feel about my story so others may find my work. Reviews really do help readers find books. Please leave a review on your favorite book site.

Don't miss out on New Releases, Exclusive Giveaways, and much more!

I'd love to hear from you directly, too. Please feel free to email me at heidisbooks999@gmail.com or check out my website at www.heidireneemason.com for updates.

Heidi Renee Mason is an Ohio girl transplanted into the Pacific Northwest. She is a people-watching introvert who can be found hiding out in the nearest corner. When not writing, she loves rainy days at the beach, old houses and antiques, researching family history, reading, and getting lost inside her own thoughts. She is a lover of caffeine and a hopeless romantic at heart. A multi-published author in the Romance genre, she moved into new writing territory in 2019 when she crossed genres. *Nothing Hidden Ever Stays*, her debut Gothic Suspense novel, became an Amazon bestseller. It was the winner of the American Fiction Award for Mystery/Suspense, as well as a Finalist in the Best Book Awards.

 twitter.com/heidireneemason

 instagram.com/authorhrmason

 bookbub.com/authors/heidi-renee-mason

ABOUT THE PUBLISHER

Hot Tree Publishing opened its doors in 2015 with an aspiration to bring quality fiction to the world of readers. With the initial focus on romance and a wide spread of romance subgenres, Hot Tree Publishing has since opened their first imprint, Tangled Tree Publishing, specializing in crime, mystery, suspense, and thriller.

Firmly seated in the industry as a leading editing provider to independent authors and small publishing houses, Hot Tree Publishing is the sister company to Hot Tree Editing, founded in 2012. Having established in-house editing and promotions, plus having a well-respected market presence, Hot Tree Publishing endeavors to be a leader in bringing quality stories to the world of readers.

Interested in discovering more amazing reads brought to you by Hot Tree Publishing? Head over to the website for information:

WWW.HOTTREEPUBLISHING.COM

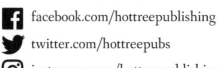

facebook.com/hottreepublishing

twitter.com/hottreepubs

instagram.com/hottreepublishing